Altered Design
Mechanical Advantage 2

By

Viola Grace

Alone on a station with only the voices in her head, Alphy needs to get in touch with the humans who are left out in space, and that means moving her ship. The trouble that she has is that the station was never designed to be flown by someone who didn't even have a driving license.

Lexo has only been out of stasis for less than a week, but he jumps at the chance to leave his sister and her lover behind to seek out the bliss of the stars once again. Programmed to rage against the enemy, he must work to keep himself calm when confronted with a woman who activates his nervous system on sight. Lust has to take a back seat to the flight of the station; he just needs to find out what the huge ship is actually designed to do.

When Alphy finds out that there have been changes made to her systems, she must face being a freak among cyborgs with her altered design.

The characters and events in this book are fictitious. Any similarity to real persons, living or dead, is coincidental and not intended by the author.

Altered Design
Copyright © 2017 by Viola Grace
ISBN: 978-1-987969-52-8

©Cover art by Carmen Waters

All rights reserved. With the exception of review, the reproduction or utilization of this work in whole or in part in any form by electronic, mechanical or other means, now known or hereafter invented, is forbidden without the express permission of the publisher.

Published by Viola Grace

Look for me online at violagrace.com, Amazon, Smashwords, Kobo, B&N and other eBook sellers.

<h1 style="text-align:center">Chapter One</h1>

S titch was yelling, Lucky was holding the package, and then, the world exploded in light and pain. Alphy was thrown back across the room, and she slammed into the wall, face first.

Alphy jerked out of the dream and rubbed her face. Again. The dream memory was rough, but her reality was rougher.

There wasn't another soul on the entire station to gossip with.

We are here. We are always here.

Alphy got up and headed into the shower, muttering, "Yeah, yeah, I know. Creepy, pervy bastards."

Vocalizing was her only way of keeping her sanity. She had woken a few years earlier with a data connection to all satellites and starships owned by Earth running through her mind. Three disembodied minds worked to sort every miniscule piece of data on staff levels, and they fed it to Alphy.

She absorbed the data, quantified it, and sorted it for distribution to the other bases. Her exposure to the outside world was over. It was just her and three brains in jars.

That is not polite, Aria. We are living beings.

You are the brain trust of the human world. You were annoying, so they sent you here, and when I got the repairs that let them put a com unit in my brain, they hooked me up with you.

We enjoy the company.

You enjoy the information.

That too.

Alphy sighed and turned off the water. *Stitch is back on the books.*

No. She is still on leave.

You made a mistake; you moved her from Medical to Base leave.

Alphy grinned as she heard the three voices muttering to find out which one had made the slip-up. She had tracked the others from Adaptation Base and connected briefly with Windy. She couldn't communicate, but she could listen. She listened in on Windy's communication with others, and she learned. It was what she had left. Information.

Reading novels from the twenty-first century took up some of her time but not enough. She worked on star maps and had the brain trust leak out the locations of Splice staging areas to the battle bases. None of them had acted on the maps until now.

Through the monitors of the barely surviving ships that the Splice had left to rot, she could see new worlds, and she wanted to get there in person.

She wrapped a towel around herself and another around her hair. The argument was still rollicking around in her mind, but the consensus was that Trell had been the one to change Stitch's classification. Onic and Duss were convinced that Trell's urge for order had taken over his sense of keeping Alphy away from her friends. It was a project of theirs. They wanted to keep her mind calm. She got excited when she spoke of and to the other ladies. The excitement made it hard for them to process through her.

She got dressed and had breakfast before walking on her rounds. The mechanical sounds of pumps and the oxygen systems were the only noise in the station. Alphy started whistling as she checked the levels in the nanite tank that housed the brains.

Why do you do that? The grumbling

came from all three voices.

Because I like it. It is silent in here. I don't have an unlimited data stream to listen to. I can't hear the sounds of the universe and the battles raging.

They grumped for a while before one said, *You need to settle in your chair. There is a conversation that you must be in on.*

She ran for the chair linked to the tank. It was the only com in or out, and since the guys couldn't speak out loud, she had no chance to do any talking. She could only send information out via data bursts embedded in the status updates. It was all filtered through the brain trust, so personal messages were out of the question.

She settled, pressed the listening tabs to her head, and leaned back, focusing on the voices she was desperate to hear in person.

One hour later, she slowly removed the tabs from her head. "Well, that was interesting. So, the Splice are attacking another race of aliens, and they need help. Oh, and Earth has cut off all supplies and support. What do you think, guys?"

The panicked shouts in her mind showed her what they were thinking. They were horrified that their usefulness and existence was coming to an end. Alphy clenched her eyes shut at the riot in her mind.

"Shut it, guys. We are going to die here unless we get to some more humans, so what do you think about taking a little road trip? There is a new species out there that needs our help. Will you work with me to help them and get some more of our own on this station?"

Everything was silent in her mind, but she could hear their whispers, even if she couldn't make them out.

Alphy called up the station manual and started to work on the propulsion unit. Cracker could have had it done in hours, but Alphy knew it was going to take her days.

Ah, well, it was something new to do, and as she knew precisely where Stitch was located, she was going to have to go to her. It couldn't be too hard to fly an asteroid, could it?

It took her three days, but she managed to prep the propulsion unit and fire up the engines. She heard the screeching of the brain trust in her mind, but she ignored them as she settled into the command chair on the main deck. Her friends were out there, and she was going to fly the database to them. The camouflage of the asteroid had been enough to keep the Splice from their door, but who knew if it would hold up while they were in motion.

Alphy was definitely willing to find out what was on the other side of the war when Earth wasn't in control.

* * * *

Stitch picked up the com. "What is it, Windy?"

Windy's voice was a strange combination of excited and amused. "You are not going to believe this."

There was a pause, and Stitch exhaled the question, "What?"

"There is an asteroid heading toward your base. I think it is Alphy."

"What do you mean?"

"I am pretty sure that the intelligence base is in motion and heading toward you right now. The satellites are picking up the movement, and the reports have stopped coming. That means that the satellites are no longer in proper position around the information station.

This is what I have worked out. What do you think?"

Stitch smiled slowly. "I think that it is a very likely situation. Do you think she can stop?"

Windy chuckled. "I fucking doubt it. If I were you, I would get a pilot up there as fast as you can. This isn't going to be pretty otherwise."

Stitch smiled and rubbed her hands together. The timing was perfect. "Thanks for the head's up. I am heading into medical. We are waking Lexo up today."

"Geez, do you think it's safe?"

"I think he will be fine. I read his file. He was put into stasis at his own request, as were the rest of those in storage. We are bringing them out one by one. I thought I would start with him."

Stitch smiled as Windy wished her good luck a moment before she signed off.

Every conversation came and went with the sudden gusts of her namesake. Windy had other folks to gossip with.

Stitch dropped the headset and returned to the underground storage and med bay. Her request to Lucky had resulted in a disarming program and modifications that would keep everyone safe, and as soon as she was at her brother's side, she would implement it.

Lexo had been a pilot before he became a weapon. She didn't want to part with him, but piloting one of their ships was an option. She wanted him happy, and she had five different plans to help him with adjusting to life out of the tank.

He had options now that the Earth had cut off the cyborg population and locked the world behind shields of weapons and satellites. The force field didn't hurt either.

Stitch walked through the corridors

until she got to the thawing space, and she nodded to Niko and Captain Blue.

"Are you ready?"

Niko scowled. "Are you sure you want to do this? He could be dangerous."

Stich touched his arm. "He *is* dangerous. I am counting on him to recognize me for who I am. Someone who cares." She patted his cheek. "I will be fine. You and Blue get out of here once the waking program is triggered."

"I don't like this." He growled it through his teeth.

"Go. I am fine. I will be fine. This is one time I am perfectly sure what I am doing." She stroked his jaw and nodded. "Now, take Blue and get out. I would rather be alone when he wakes. My decision, my brother, my risk."

Blue snorted. "The cycle is starting. We have a minute before he is up to temperature. Come on, Nikolai. Let's get out of here."

The beeping and chirping ceased, and whirring started. Stitch squeezed Niko's hand and walked toward the canister. When the lid opened, she was alone, and Lexo was asleep inside. His chest was lifting and dropping, and she stroked his head out of reflex.

He grimaced and then gave her a small smile. "I am still going to enlist, Stephanie."

She sighed, and tears tracked down her cheeks. "I think I might sign up as well, Lexo. Mom and Dad are going to freak out."

She paused. "In fact, I already did."

He opened his eyes and stared. "You are older."

"I am. It has been more than nine years, Lexo. You have been asleep for three of them."

He raised his hand to her cheek, and he jolted. "The implants. Get back; I am dangerous."

"They have been nullified. We can get you into the repair unit upstairs, and it can work on giving you more control."

He looked at her, and he clenched his hand as he lowered it to his side. "You should have left me to rot. Earth will never have me back."

She chuckled and got right to the point. "They won't have any of us back. It is quite the story. So, get out of bed, put on these clothes, and I will take you to the base itself. I have some folks for you to meet and a story to tell."

He struggled to get out of the stasis unit, and she helped him as she had helped dozens of men in recovery. Her brother was alive, he knew who she was, and he had covered his junk. When she added the impending arrival of Alphy, the day was pretty good.

Chapter Two

Alphy watched the reports from the short-range satellites spinning around the intelligence station. The nearest Splice were too far away to see her, and the base was getting nearer with every passing hour. She should be able to see it in just over a week.

The guys had stopped screaming at her over their new destination and were sullen as they took in the information from the satellites about the surrounding system.

The three battle zones they had passed through on their journey had finally made the situation real for the strategic command. They were alone.

Bodies of men were out there in the black, and ships had been shattered in confrontations. No one was safe if the Splice were roaming the area.

Alphy was checking the trajectory toward the battle base when an incoming alert echoed through the facility.

"Shit, shit, shit, shit, shit." She tried to find out which sensors had given the alert, but the intruder alarm sounded before she could.

She got to her feet and sprinted for the weapons' locker. Alphy wasn't really good with weapons, but the new targeting system that had been designed into her implants increased her chances of hitting a target exponentially.

Every bit of experimental enhancement to human cognition was at her disposal, so she downloaded stealth techniques and brought up the interior schematic of the station. She had to protect the brains, and that meant the junction of the only two corridors that led the way.

With three large weapons that were point-and-shoot by design, she sprinted down the halls to get to that junction. They might be annoying, but they were hers to protect. She might want to kill them, but no one else was allowed to.

The cheering in her mind was hushed when she growled at them. She needed all her concentration for keeping her newly downloaded battle skills in place.

The link to the station showed her the entry point. The intruder was in one of the shuttle bays and heading her way.

She pulled the gun into a firing position and kept heading for the split in the hallway.

* * * *

Lexo grimaced. According to Stitch, Alphy was an officious nerd who liked to organize data more than anything else. He didn't anticipate too much of a fight. They were on the same side, after all.

The station seemed empty. His footfalls echoed in the halls as he headed for the command centre, and no other sounds were heard. It was eerie.

Checking the propulsion for this monstrosity was his first job. Getting it under his control was the second.

The surreal situation that he was in brought a smile to his lips. He hadn't imagined that his sister would have entered the war and definitely wouldn't have thought that she would be in charge of a base. Getting ordered around by his little sister had been weird enough, but seeing all the fighters that she had doing her bidding had been a shock.

The alien contingent was also something that took getting used to. They looked so close to human at first glance that it wasn't until you saw the wings that your brain filled in the gap.

He walked through the halls, thinking about how useful flying would be as an adaptation, completely relaxed and introspective. The bolt of energy that slammed into the wall near his head was a bit of a surprise.

Lexo tucked, rolled, and shielded himself with a corner. "I am guessing you are Alphy."

There was a pause. "You are human." The voice was definitely female.

"Sort of. Would it matter if I said Stitch sent me?" He waited for three beats of his replaced heart.

"How do I know that?"

"Because she is bossy, smart, and my sister. I am her brother, Lexo. They just thawed me out." As he chatted with her, his targeting system was telling him where to shoot and how to kill. He ignored it.

"Why are you here?"

"Because they don't want you to crash into the Adaptation Base. I am a pilot."

Weapons clattered to the ground for so long he wondered if they were all she was wearing. There seemed to be enough to cover a whole body.

"I am not a pilot. My name is Alphy. I have put down my guns."

He slowly straightened and kept his hands at his sides. "I am coming around the corner."

"Okay."

He turned the corner and faced her, blinking in surprise at the tiny beast that had almost blown his brains out.

A bodysuit wrapped her curves from ankle to collarbone, and she was definitely female. The silver line across her forehead made him pause. "Head injury?"

She wrinkled her nose. "Oh, yes. Same incident that blew your sister's arms up."

"Blew... She's a cyborg?" He blinked. It hadn't occurred to him to actually *look* at her. Her face was still hers, and that is what he had been looking at. His little sister, all grown up.

"Yeah. They tried to kill us. They nearly succeeded."

He looked her straight in the face, taking in the bright swirl of colour in her eyes and the detailed edge of the join between metal and flesh. "You were hurt as well."

She snorted. "Come with me, and I will explain things. I just need to get some confirmations from the database."

"Of course. I have a message packet from my sister as well."

"Good. Bring that too." She gathered her weapons and stalked down the hall, leaving him to watch her curvy backside as it swayed in front of him. It had been nearly a decade since he had been this close to a woman, and the light scent in the air made his eyes narrow as he inhaled to memorize it.

The woman stiffened. "Dude, if you are sniffing me, I am going to write your sister a scathing letter."

Lexo grinned and watched her back as she led him through the station. Flying this monster was going to be interesting, but the company was good.

* * * *

Alphy clutched the weapons and led him through the station to her private grotto. The moment that he crossed the threshold, a laser cage sprang up and out from all sides of the garden.

"What the hell?"

She turned and looked over her shoulder. "I am just going to check your credentials, and then, you will be free to go."

He scowled as he stood with his arms crossed and legs splayed. "What happens if I don't?"

She shrugged, "Your cage gets very small, very fast, and then bots clean up the mess. Hang tight. I will be back in a few minutes."

She walked back to the armoury and got two pistols, settling them on her thighs and tying the holsters into place. She didn't know what was going on, but she needed to find out.

The data stream told her what she needed to know. Captain Lexo Carter was indeed back on duty. After years of being in stasis, Stitch had woken him up and applied a few new programs.

When Alphy read his history, her eyes widened, though they were blind to the physical world.

He was a prototype. She had thought that they all died in the early days of the war against the Splice, but here he was, on her station and in her prison.

His programming had been basic. He had been given a nanite override to do his best to keep the war effort moving forward. When he had been assigned to a suicide mission with his men, he had simply killed the general giving the order. No commander meant no command that would take out his men on a mission that couldn't be won. The war effort required a different tactic, and the command needed to find it.

After the murder, he had been court martialled with the result being that he was not guilty of insubordination. He had followed the programming set to him by Earth Command. Unlike any of the other men fighting, the prototype cyborgs literally had no other option. The nanites made them carry out the programmed protocols.

She moved past the records and disciplinary hearing that ended with his request for stasis. Alphy was looking for details on his flying skills.

Whoa. Huh, so the only thing that he couldn't fly was a paper airplane. Anything made in the last hundred years had been in his list of familiar machines. Lexo had been an aviation fanatic before he became a cyborg, and it hadn't stopped just because he was missing a few limbs.

"Well, I guess he can do the job." She removed her tabs and sat up.

"I am so glad you think so." Lexo's voice came from her left.

She sat up in her cradle and stared at him. "How did you get out?"

"My family designed more than just the cyborg program. We also dabbled in defense systems. No projected laser can go through a mirror." He held up his wrist. A small reflective circle on his skin flashed as he moved his arm.

She swung her legs out of the cradle and got to her feet. "You killed your commanding officer."

"I did. He was ordering his team to commit suicide for no purpose other than his own ego. That countered the directives that were controlling my system at the time."

"Are you still bound by that?"

"No, Stephanie had the protocols removed. It is all in the data packet I am carrying."

"Steph—oh, right. Stitch. Good. She does usually think of everything to get the most out of her patients." Alphy rubbed her arms.

The cheerful menace of her guest was unmistakable, but his credentials had checked out. He had flown mission after mission, bringing the maximum number of men back to the base. His willingness to wait for the last batch of retreating warriors had not gone down well with his superiors. The devotion to his missions had been all-consuming, and now, he was assigned to her.

The triplets were shrieking in her thoughts, and she grabbed her temple while holding onto the barrier that wrapped around the data cradle.

"Is something wrong?"

"I am just being yelled at for not shooting you. They will get over it once I put in the authorizations."

"By whom?"

She laughed. "We are definitely not the reason for this asteroid. Just let me get you to the command deck, and you can try to steer this turkey to Stitch's base."

He nodded. "Fine. I will address the issue of the cage at a later time."

She wrinkled her nose. "You do that. I am more than willing to excuse your unannounced incursion onto my base."

Lexo was surprised. "I suppose that is

true."

"Yeah. Let's just suppose that." She straightened and ignored the inner squabbling, walking nonchalantly past the tank that held the minds of the three screaming idiots.

"What's this?"

She should have known that one of Stitch's siblings would have keen intuition. "It is classified for now. Once we get to the base, I am sure that you will learn all the ins and outs of the rock."

He was behind her with all the subtlety of a warm wall. "Lead the way."

She didn't comment but hiked away from the accumulated information of the Earth forces and led Lexo to what was going to be his domain. He could steer, she would read, they didn't have to bump into each other more than that.

Chapter Three

" Hiya, Alphy. I hope this finds you well." Stitch's familiar face waved a silvered hand to the camera.

Alphy smiled and fought the urge to wave back.

"So, if you are watching this, you have met my brother, Lexo. He isn't as irritating as he seems, he is just really straightforward in his thinking. And yes, I know he can probably hear me."

Stitch grinned and winked, "Now, if you are the one on that asteroid, then you are heading for me, and I am delighted. My brother was one of what appears to be thousands of cyborgs who were taken offline."

Alphy was shocked, but she shouldn't have been. That kind of data is exactly what the brains were trying to keep from her.

"I have been in touch with Windy and Lucky. Apparently, Cracker designed our parts when no one else was up for it. I haven't heard much from Lacey yet, but I know she is around. Two slow-moving cases have arrived with coffee and chocolate. There is only one person who would make that a priority." Stitch laughed and then she sobered.

"Right. We need to start making a plan. I have met aliens that look like us. Like seriously look like us, but they have huge dragonfly wings and can actually use them for propulsion. They follow orders way better than the human guys do, but coming from a matriarchal society, they have an inborn respect for women in charge."

Alphy grinned at the thought.

"Stop smirking, Alphy. Lexo is going to be a pain in the ass to deal with, but if the math was right, you still have a week or more with him. He's a good pilot, and he takes his job seriously. You are in good hands. I will see you soon, and we can have a good laugh at our changes together."

Stitch paused. "One more thing. Thanks for surviving. It means a lot."

The screen went blank, and Alphy smiled, brushing at the tears in her eyes.

She exhaled and looked over to where Lexo was under the command controls, his trunk-like legs sticking out from under the console.

How had the same genetics that made the lithe and delicate Stitch come up with the hulk that was her brother?

She walked over to where he was working and sat on the floor. "So, what is your family like?"

He paused in his rewiring. "They are

focused on their studies."

"How many brothers and sisters?"

"I have three sisters, including Stephanie, and one other brother. My parents were researchers in nanite technology, and my brother was in the weapons research and development area."

"What about your sisters?"

"Ah, they were all in various medical fields. Stitch focused on the repair and replacement of limbs for natural function. We had no idea that our careers would suddenly become our lives."

"What did you do as a career?"

He chuckled from under the shroud covered with wires and metal. "Aircraft. Every kind of aircraft that I could find, I took to the skies. What did you do before the attacks?"

"Administration. I can fill out paperwork for, and find bits of useful information in, just about anything. I was requisitioning stuff that the supply station didn't know it had to outfit the bases. Each outpost was set up to remain on its own for ten years minimum, and they didn't even know it."

She sighed. "You are the first person I have spoken to since the explosion."

He paused and pulled himself out from under the console. "You are kidding."

She shrugged. "Not really. I woke up here after the surgery to repair my head, and there was not another soul here."

"How long has it been?"

"Three years. I don't know how long it was before that. It could have been weeks or months. Things were a little hazy until they were able to patch my skull."

She could see the lines of scarring on his face. It was natural healing that would have occurred before the nanites were invited into his system. The stubble made her blink. She hadn't seen facial hair in decades.

She had to stop herself from reaching out to touch his cheek.

He shifted and leaned against the side of the open panel. "What happened there?"

"It was an attempt to cripple the war effort by Splice sympathizers. The idiots thought that the Splice could be reasoned with if we sacrificed our own lower classes to them."

Lexo's shock was apparent. "What?"

"Yeah. You heard me. They wanted to feed the lowest of income families to the Splice. Safe at home, they knew better than those who have actually seen the monsters we are fighting." She shrugged.

"What happened to them?"

"They were found and tried by the United Earth court for sabotage, and their sentences were sealed. No one out here knows what happened to them. The rumour is that they were sentenced to death, but I don't believe it. That kind tends to wriggle out from under this sort of thing. They use money to grease the wheels."

Lexo let out a low sound that appeared to be a growl. "I want to find out what happened."

"Me too, but they didn't broadcast the result, so there isn't any way for us to find out what went on." She shrugged. It wasn't precisely true. If the brain trust would let her, she could break through the tech walls that had been set up. Alphy had all the codes, she just needed the access. She had tried twice, but the collective had shut her down—literally. She had woken in her cradle and had been ordered to keep her mind on their brains and on the station requisitions.

Lexo grunted. "Right. If I ever find out who tried to blow up my sister, they will regret that I am not bound by the old programming."

Alphy nodded. "Right. Why did you agree to that?"

He gave her a bland look. "I woke up with it after my first crash, and it was set in me, carried to the implant for my ear injury."

"And from there to the brain."

"Right. Well, I had better get back to work."

"What are you doing?" She shifted to her knees.

"I am rewiring the propulsion systems to work with my adaptations. The system was halfway there already. Your handiwork?"

She smiled. "I had to get it moving somehow. I read the manual and bypassed the security controls."

He looked surprised. "You did a good job. Very neat."

"Thanks. Well, I will leave you to it. Let me know when you want to be shown to your quarters."

He nodded. "You enjoyed Stephanie's note?"

Alphy grinned. "It was great. I just wish I could send a communication back."

He winked. "Give me a few days. First, I want to start putting on a bit of speed."

"Excellent. I will be in the cradle and listening to the chatter. Time to earn my rations."

She stood and headed back to the communications centre near the tank. The information coming in was now of deliberate interest to her. She wanted to know what the other bases were doing now that they were cut off from their home.

Onic, Duss, and Trell were pouting.

She closed her eyes and put her tabs on, looking for the information she wanted.

He isn't authorized to be here.

I know. I need him to fly the ship.

We should not have left our posting. We were safe there.

What good would it do to have all this knowledge and no one to speak to?

It is our knowledge to keep.

No, it is humanity's knowledge, and I am more human than you are right now, so I win. So, leave Lexo alone and don't send the bots to do anything weird to him.

We would never!

You did it to me.

There was rumbling, and Trell muttered, *We are sorry. He is different.*

He is a pilot. He will bring us close to the base without crashing us. I got us moving; he will set us in at a safe distance. I wouldn't know how or where to stop.

Yet, you put us on this path.

She sighed. *It had to be done. With Earth out of our reach, we have to come up with a new plan for survival. I know it doesn't matter to you, but the rest of us are still being driven to live and flourish, not to mention pushing the Splice back into the hell they crawled out of.*

The pompous tone was a triad of mansplaining that had echoed through the centuries. *The majority of the cyborg population are males. They can't flourish, let alone, grow.*

There are at least six ladies out here. That's a start. There is also an alien race involved now, and they might be a close-enough match with a bit of genetic fiddling.

We need to discuss it.

Silence fell as the minds muttered and mumbled in the corners of her thoughts.

Alphy enjoyed the silence and continued her journey through the reports that had been filed in the last days of active communication with home.

The information that she gleaned was interesting. There had been a sudden technical surge in the months before the lockdown. It was either a breakthrough, or the researchers had gotten information from somewhere other than Earth. She made a mental note to keep looking for records of the new tech and continued her information gathering.

"How long are you going to stay there?"

She blinked and sat up slowly, removing the connecting tabs. "I am done."

Alphy tried to get to her feet, but she swayed and fell back into the molded support.

Lexo was at her side in an instant, and he helped her to her feet. "Sorry, I didn't mean to jolt you."

"Is the wiring done?"

He nodded. "I was done hours ago and went looking for you when I got hungry."

"Oh, of course. Sorry. The unit is this way."

She tried to ease free of his grip on her arm, but he came with her and continued to offer himself as a balance point.

The commissary was a large and empty expanse, the nutrition units were designed to scan whatever human tissue you could present to it for a meal to match your needs.

"This place is designed for thousands. How many folks are here?"

"Um, just me. This was a silent station for most of the war. I was posted here after the explosion at the Adaptation Base."

"So, you have been alone all this time?" Lexo's voice was suddenly concerned.

"More or less. I don't really mind the solitude, but I miss the base. There was always someone around at the base." She walked him to the dispenser and activated the scanner.

The machine chirped and whirred as it selected her meal and rolled it onto the tray. The tray moved down the belt, and she went with it.

Lexo followed her example and took in the full scan. His hands had been replaced as had a few patches on his arms and torso. The pause in the beam was proof of where the adaptations were.

She held her questions until they were at a table with a flask of tea and a carafe of water. Her first actual person to talk to and now she had to decide where to start.

Chapter Four

With her first dinner companion in years, she found she didn't know how to start.

After discarding three topics, she finally asked him, "Why did you join up?"

He paused to swallow. "I come from a long line of researchers, but I didn't match any of them. I can work in a lab, but it isn't my true passion. I have always been fascinated by aeronautics, so that is what I went after. My family encouraged it, but when we were attacked, it was all hands to the research facility. I chose a different direction. They went in, I went out."

"Wow. You were in the first defenders?"

He nodded. "I already had flight control implants, so I was in on the initial defense. First, we stayed near Earth and gradually pushed the Splice back."

Alphy nodded. "The first defenders did good work."

He smiled slightly. "We took care of our own."

She sipped at her water glass and smiled as she put it down.

Lexo cocked his head. "Why did you join up?"

She rubbed the back of her neck. "I didn't. I was caught in the first Splice raid and never went home again."

He froze. "What?"

"You heard me. I ended up on a Splice ship... in the storage area. They took us out one by one, and no one came back. It was a relief when the ship was rocked to the side and we heard the air escaping." She finished her meal.

He was staring at her. "What?"

"I was on a Splice vessel when they were seeing how good a match we were. I lost sixteen friends in two days. We had been on a work excursion in the capitol. We were there to look at human history and ended up becoming a foot-note."

"There weren't any survivors of the first incursion."

She shrugged. "There were four of us. We got off without a scratch while others were harvested for parts. It wasn't a particularly fun time."

"How did you get free?"

"We waited and prepared to die. The air seeped out, and it got cold." She stared down at her water glass as she remembered. "We were all in separate cages when they came for us. The Splice came to us, some wearing the skin and limbs of humans of every shade. They opened our cages and hauled us out, pushing us in front of them as we stumbled through the halls. Their language still grates in my thoughts."

"They spoke to you?" He leaned forward eagerly.

"They spoke to each other. We didn't know what was going on."

"How did you escape?"

She blinked slowly. "We didn't. They took us to the dissection room where others were still screaming, and they hooked us up to individual headgear. The switch was flipped, everything went bright, and I woke up on an orbital station six months later. I still don't know how I made it out or how the others did."

"You said there were four survivors?"

"Yes, as far as I know, there are now two. Two of the others killed themselves within two days of their regaining consciousness."

Lexo was horrified. "Killed themselves? What did they do to you?”

She shrugged. “We still don’t know. There has been a change to my brain chemistry, but my cognition works the same as it always has.”

“What about the other survivor?”

Alphy shrugged. “She was moved to another facility before I woke up.”

Lexo leaned back. “Wow. That makes my tales of daring look a little tame.”

She shrugged. “I survived and then I survived again. It beat the alternative.”

Silence settled in between them.

“What do you remember about the explosion? Stephanie won’t say much about it.”

Alphy closed her eyes. “It was a birthday party for Lucky. We—the ladies from the administrative end of things—loved having an excuse to get together. Anyone who did five minutes of research would know that when a birthday rolled around, they would have an opportunity.”

She smiled slightly. “Lucky had just opened a silk negligee and was blushing furiously when the next box was set next to her. Stitch must have seen something in the tag because she called a warning. The next thing anyone knew, we were blasted into the walls, and Cracker was calling for help.”

“So, none of you have normal names?”

She snorted. “We were at a military base. We used the nicknames for immediate emotional connection. It worked with co-workers and patients alike.”

He settled back again, a bit more at ease with this topic. “What was my sister like at the base?”

Alphy grinned. “Stitch could look at a patient and create a treatment plan in minutes. She not only advocated for what was best for the patient, but also what would make him a more effective cyborg. Implanting weapons was an activity of last resort, but she always had the full roster of equipment and skills set into the nanites before they were set about their tasks. She is a great assessment officer, so I make sure she has what she needs."

"That last bit was in present tense."

Alphy chuckled. "Manipulating the raw material shipments for the fabricators is still under my purview. Monitoring data is what this station was built for, so I do my work through the automated systems. It took some practice, but now, I can move supplies anywhere I need them to be."

"Is that what you were doing in that chair?"

She blinked and smirked. "Sure. Sounds plausible."

He cocked his head. "Well, now that I know where to eat, what else is there to do on this station?"

"Name it, and we have it. You can learn to knit or engage in hand-to-hand combat with solid light simulations that your nanites react to, and everything in between."

"Well, show me where the facilities are, and I will get started figuring out what I want to do."

Alphy nodded and got to her feet, taking her tray to the recycler. Lexo followed her and mimicked her precisely. When the dishes were dealt with, she led the way to the crew quarters, and she asked, "How far down to you want to be?"

"Across from you is fine. I don't want to infringe on your freedoms, but if we are the only two living beings on this monstrous ship, I want to stay close."

"This is weird. I have bcen alone here a long time."

"That is over now. You had better get ready for a lot more company."

Alphy blinked. "What?"

"You are in possession of a long-range spacecraft with natural gravity. Stephanie has plans that involve us travelling to collect the other cyborgs who are stuck on their bases and bringing them here." Lexo chuckled. "It is quite the project, and it is going to involve a lot of flying."

"Speaking of flying, aren't you supposed to be doing that?"

"I am. I set the linkage between me and the station engines. I can control the trajectory in my sleep if I have to." He smiled and rubbed his jaw.

She stared for a moment, and he stopped to look at her.

"What?"

"I haven't seen facial hair in quite a while."

He wrinkled his nose. "Sorry. No stations pack razors anymore, and my primer nanites were first gen, so the shaving protocol hadn't been added."

"Don't apologize. It is just going to take some getting used to." She laughed and resumed walking, "Would you believe my legs are in a similar state?"

He chuckled and drew up next to her. "No, but thanks for the commonality."

She grinned. "Good. So, you have a cranial adaptation, is there anything else?"

"I thought you read my file."

"I did, but it is always nice to tell your own story."

He sighed. "Cranial, spinal, bone replacements in both arms, a hip, and one leg."

She whistled softly. "Ouch. Sound like crash injuries."

"You are very good. Yes, I had to use my ship as a ram on a few occasions, and there were few restraints to hold me back."

"Did you ever confront the Splice

face-to-whatever?"

"On a few occasions. I only went out when we had another pilot on hand; otherwise, I kept the engines ready to run."

That didn't match with what she had read. "You were weaponized."

"I was. Solo missions in small shuttles. I went in, disabled the Splice ship and destroyed anything on the way. They weren't my favourite moments, but this is war. There shouldn't be any moments that you treasure."

He cocked his head. "There might be a few. Life has to spark, or there isn't any reason to fight. Now, what adaptations do you have?"

She sighed. It was only fair. "A fair amount of my skull and brain is artificial, as is my spine. I was blasted into the wall, and my head took the bulk of the impact. They got the nanites in while I was on the gurney, and the data transfer took place before too many cells could die. It was similar to a bad hangover by the time I woke up.”

“Do you know why it took so long for Stephanie to wake up?”

She sighed. “I have a few theories but nothing concrete. They kept her in stasis until they needed her. That’s all I can guess.”

“What would they need her for?”

“What indeed? Why would you need an expert on assessing what folks needed to be alive and functioning normally and naturally right as we were exposed to a new species?”

“They couldn’t have known.”

She muttered, “Someone did.” A moment later, she perked up, “Right, these are my quarters.”

He laughed. “You are in the captain’s quarters?”

“Why not?”

“Very well. I will take the second-in-command's quarters across the way."

"Did you want to settle in tonight, or did you want to continue the tour?"

Lexo sighed, "I would like to continue the tour. The schematics are one thing, but seeing it first hand is far more useful."

"Right. Well, clothing is accessible through the fabrication station in your quarters or at the gym."

"Great. What about medical checks? I am still not used to the alterations that Stephanie made in my implants. They feel like they aren't there anymore."

"Well, we have a firing zone where you can work with what is left in your system. Oh, did you see any of the aliens?"

"Yes. I saw several of them in various stages of repair."

She moved closer to him and whispered, "Do they really have wings?"

He gave her a stern look. "How do

you know that?"

Alphy made a face. "The parts requested for fabrication. There are very few implants possible that would need that kind of a bladed strut for support, as well as the socket joint that would be strong enough to support a few hundred pounds."

He whistled. "Interesting assessment. You really do know the inventories like the back of your hand."

Alphy shrugged. "It is what I do. It is what I have always done. It's what I am good at."

She paused. "The door is primed for you. You just need to stand in front of it so it can scan you."

Her door glowed a soft blue, and his was a vivid purple.

He smiled, stepped to the door and allowed the scan. The door opened for him, and he stepped inside. He let out that low whistle again. "This is more room than I had back on Earth."

She smiled and leaned on the wall. "Yeah, it would be a shame to waste all the extra space and keep to the crew quarters."

He finished looking around and joined her again. "So, where to next?"

"Exercise or entertainment?"

"Exercise. I have been asleep for a few years, so I need to work the kinks out of the system."

"Okay. Come with me. I am pretty sure that we can manage any kink you can come up with." She smiled and then blushed when he raised a brow. "You know what I mean."

He grinned. "I do, but I like the way yours sounded."

Her blush lasted the entire twenty-minute walk to the recreation area.

Chapter Five

The fabrication scanner was set up for her, so she quickly got her exercise gear made, and then, she stepped aside while it generated.

"Have you used one of these before?"

He nodded. "At the Alpha Base."

"Just relax and don't tense up. As long as your feet are lined up right, the exercise suit won't interfere with your junk."

He snorted and locked his heels against the stops designed for that purpose.

The scanner hummed and took in all of his contours, top to bottom.

While he was being scanned, she collected her suit and wandered around the corner to the changing area. Her baggy uniform was discarded, and she pulled on the form-fitting, sleeveless exercise suit.

She was dressed and pulling her hair up into a restraint clip when he came around the corner.

Lexo paused. "You... look like you are in good shape."

She glanced down and had to crane her neck to see her feet. "I try to be. A healthy body goes a long way to keeping you able to act in whatever means necessary."

"You definitely look healthy."

She grimaced. "Right. I will see you on the workout floor."

Her enthusiasm for her new companion paled at his obvious shock. Her curves were a throwback to a previous era when women were designed to attract at a glance, rather than through the online brokers that matched folks based on goals and genetics.

Her uniform usually camouflaged her body. It was baggy and turned her into the same block as the delicate women of ethereal construction that were so popular on contemporary Earth. If the Splice hadn't snagged her, she would still have been destined to be alone. Her body type was dying out strictly because it was unfashionable in the global market.

She set up a boxing station and started to work on the heavy bag, remembering that it was what had made the Adaptation Base feel like home. Most of the women there had the same exaggerated curves that she did.

"You have a good form."

Alphy screamed and whirled to face him. Her mind recognized him and told her to stand down. She leaned forward and put her palms on her thighs. "Damn. I forgot you were here."

He blinked in surprise. "Sorry. You really have been here for quite a while on your own."

"Yeah. For six months, I pretended that this station was haunted, just so I could talk out loud." She pressed her hand to her chest to calm the thundering beat.

She inhaled and straightened. "Right. Where did you want to start?"

She stared at him, surprised by the smooth silver skin that marched along his arms as well as the extent of the silver skin down his right side. From what she had learned, most modern cyborgs enjoyed turning their nanites into tattoos using a subroutine that Lucky had crafted.

"I think I would enjoy a bit of wrestling if you can show me how to set up the unit." The silvery skin of his arms flexed.

"No problem. This way, please." She

smiled politely and led the way to the projection unit.

Alphy showed him how to calibrate the unit, and he was far too close to her while she did. The heat coming from him was amazing, and she fought the urge to lean back against him. He was her pilot, nothing more.

Once he was sure of the controls, she left him to get to work and returned to her pummelling the heavy bag.

She could blank her mind when she was working out, and even the Triad couldn't break in.

When her arms were humming from the exertion and she was coated in a sheen of sweat, she paused and held onto the bag while looking toward the wrestling mat.

Lexo was facing off with the solid-light hologram. His skin was glowing with sweat, and he had obviously taken a few trips to the mat.

The program was using the most recent of Lucky's programs, and it looked like she had done one helluva job.

Lexo rushed forward and collided with his projected opponent. The nanites in his system forced his muscles to treat the projection as a real being. The calibration that set the machine also set Lexo.

The bulge of muscles was impressive, and Alphy watched as the real and the projected man grappled and fought for the upper hand.

As she watched, he was lifted, turned, and slammed to the ground. The scoreboard totalled the current tally at three wins to the projection and one to Lexo.

Lexo fought for air and slowly levered himself to his feet, returning to the start position and waiting.

Alphy wanted to step in, but she waited until the next bout of attack and retreat ended with Lexo on the ground again, pushed out of the ring.

"I think that you need a bit of training before you set it to expert again." She walked over and crouched next to him.

Lexo grimaced. "That is one hell of a simulation."

Alphy grinned. "Yeah, it is one of her best. I don't get beyond amateur in most of her simulations, but the wrestling program has me at beginner and still kicks my ass."

He groaned and sat up. "You know the designer?"

"Sure. She worked with me and Stitch. Lucky is the best at writing code that works with nanites. The machines here compensate for your adaptations and give you human reflexes and strength, or it reacts like you do. It gets stronger to make up the difference."

He gave her a long look. "You don't know how it works, do you?"

She shrugged. "Not one hundred percent positive. Since I can't ask Lucky any questions, I have to guess by the application of the programs."

"What is the reason that you can't communicate?"

Alphy chuckled. "Ah, this is the repository station. I can't send anything out for fear that the Splice will trace it back and learn all of humanity's secrets."

Lexo leaned his arms on his knees. He held up his silver hand and flexed it. "Are we still human?"

"I think so. I still want my world to survive, even if they changed the locks."

He grinned. "Sound thinking. Yeah, I want the rest of my family to live long and happy lives, even if I can't be there."

He got to his feet and wiped the sweat from his brow with the back of his hand.

"What other delights are there to experiment with?" He raised his brows.

She led him to the control panel and showed him the options. Now that he had been calibrated, he just needed to do a palm scan at the station he wanted, and the machine would configure itself for him.

Alphy went for a cardio workout and started a light sprint that turned into a run. With her adaptations had come increased reflexes and the urge to keep fit. It wasn't something she had dealt with before, so she chalked it up to the changes after the explosion and did as her body requested.

She would probably have an answer as to why her repaired body had an agenda of its own, but she needed to be able to speak to someone for that, and the guys weren't forthcoming as to what precisely had happened to her body when she was injured. She had a good idea, but she couldn't be positive until someone told her the truth. No one seemed interested in that information.

Exhausted, she headed to her quarters while Lexo continued to work out. The change in satellite feeds that she could sense was a good sign. They were passing through monitored space, and that usually meant that humans had been somewhere close.

In a matter of days, she would be with her own people again. Stitch was going to be hugged to within an inch of her life.

Chapter Six

*S*he was trapped. She couldn't move her body. Her mind was awake, but none of her other senses worked. She was screaming, but she couldn't make a sound.

Hands shook her, and she fought the grip. She was held tighter, and as her senses came back online, her sobs were harsh to her own ears. Lexo held her to his chest while she cried as her body woke one sense at a time.

When her activation cycle had run its course, she sniffled and slid a hand between them to wipe her face. "Sorry to wake you."

"I am a light sleeper, so not much can

get past me. What was that all about?"

She shivered and inhaled the warm scent of him. "It happens every six months or so. I forgot I was up for a reset with the excitement of your arrival."

"Reset?"

"My system gets a bulk update from the archive, but in order to do that, it has to take my body offline."

"What archive?"

She paused and sniffled again. He hugged her tighter.

"What archive, Alphy?"

The three minds in hers were surprisingly quiet.

"Uh, the Earth Archive. That is what this place is. It is everything that every human has known, thought, and recorded since we have been keeping printed words and online archives." She chuckled against his chest. "We have every video ever made somewhere in this station."

"Why doesn't anyone know about this place?"

She turned her face toward his, "Because this is the last bit of humanity to hold against the Splice. Even if they get us all, they can't wipe us out completely. This station has tendrils all over space. Each satellite holds a link that goes dead if the Splice board it. Lights have been winking out in the stars. They are looking for us."

He leaned back, and his lips were nearly touching hers. "Who is *us?*"

She held her breath, but the voices spoke.

Bring him.

Bring him.

Bring him.

"I think they are up to meeting you." She smiled tightly and tried to get loose. Lexo was still holding her.

"I believe you might want to get dressed first. It has been a while, and my self-control isn't what it should be."

She became aware of the press of skin on skin and the slight slide of sweat between them. Her reboot always left her drenched in sweat, but now, she wasn't the only witness.

"Um, I will get dressed as soon as you let me go."

Lexo slowly released her, as if reluctant to do so.

A quick glance told her that she wasn't the only one who slept naked. Also, she wasn't the only one who had been enjoying the embrace.

She scooted around him and grabbed for one of the men's t-shirts that she had commandeered. It fell to her knees, and she was covered enough for most human societies in a matter of seconds. The robe she threw on was due to Lexo and the cooler air around the tank.

Lexo left while she dressed, and when she entered her doorway, he was wearing some exercise pants and flexible boots. Nothing else.

Alphy exhaled, nodded, and led the way. "They are just past the cradle you found me in."

"What is that thing?"

"All in good time." She chuckled and stiffened her shoulders. She was about to break a bazillion protocols, but if the guys wanted to meet him, she was happy to make the introductions.

Lexo wasn't the type to fill in the gaps with idle chitchat, and Alphy was used to being alone. She hiked through the station until they were next to her information station.

She turned sharply and headed down the optically hidden staircase. If you didn't know it was there, you would never see it.

"They are this way."

"This... how did I miss this?"

She chuckled and moved through the

familiar path. "You weren't looking for it."

Alphy brought him to the edge of the tank, and she leaned against the railing. "Here they are. The three smartest and most obnoxious brain donors in human history."

"Brain?"

She waited, and the silvery liquid stirred. Onic's body rose from the silver, his brain visible through the constructed shape.

"Welcome to our humble home, pilot. I am Onic, first of the Triad of Advisory and the living human archive."

Trell and Duss formed out of the nanites and stood on the rippling surface.

The choice of Grecian style robes made Alphy snicker.

"I am Trell, second of the Triad."

"I am Duss, third, and best looking of the Triad."

Lexo stared and cocked his head. "You are three brains without bodies."

The Triad nodded.

Lexo cleared his throat. "Why don't you just have the nanites generate bodies?"

Alphy grinned. She had asked that question a few times herself.

Duss scowled. "The physical bodies cannot contain our knowledge. Only the mix of the liquid nanites and our minds can maintain the vast knowledge of human kind."

Alphy chuckled. "That is what they say. I am pretty sure it is just so that they can switch outfits on a whim. They just stay swimming brains for me. You are lucky."

Lexo looked at her with sudden understanding. "This is *us*."

"Correct. They are my only companions. Well, they were until you showed up."

"Glad to be of service. Now, why does Alphy need to be here?"

Alphy waited for the response. She could hear the murmurs in the part of her brain that they occupied. She was their link to the outside world, such as it was.

Onic smiled slightly. "She is our link to the outside world. She is also our caretaker and our reminder of what it is to be human. We were in danger of being lost in the histories and information until she arrived. Now that we are linked to her, it is a much more purposeful universe ahead of us."

Alphy looked at his representation with surprise. "That's flattering."

He shrugged. "It is the truth. Our link to you has caused us to view the world—the human race—in a light we had nearly forgotten."

Lexo asked, "How long have you been like this?"

Trell shrugged his shoulders. "We have been in space for over seventy years. We were out here long before the Splice came to Earth."

Onic nodded. "Our knowledge is to be kept safe for the reference of future generations."

Duss's nearly transparent features smiled. "We sensed that an alien incursion would not be too far away, and after we notified the ruling bodies, we set about creating this ship."

Lexo looked around. "This was all built before the Splice?"

Onic chuckled. "Of course. There would have been no way to move us after the attack. We had to move while it was safe and no one would notice. As we had all been in different facilities around the world, we merely had ourselves shipped up here and placed into the tank. The nanites were programmed to take care of our particular needs."

Duss nodded, "It was easy to create this station, this ship. What was difficult was finding someone who could communicate with us without using a display system. When Aria was injured, it was the perfect time to adjust her adaptations and have her sent here."

Alphy blinked. "I didn't know that you tinkered with me."

Trell waved his manifested hand as if it didn't matter. "There were alterations to your design that were necessary for the situation we had in mind for you. Using you as a data filter to add emotional weight to the information has been most useful."

Onic chimed in. "With your view point, we were able to get the troops to safe stations before Earth could seal itself. Everyone has a place to call home, in one way or another."

She blushed. "I didn't..."

Lexo looked from her to the three

floating brains in silvery masculine forms. "You pull the data through her, you reboot her to purge her systems, and you have had her here alone. You are some sick bastards."

Alphy blinked. "It's fine. My body was broken in a bunch of places. I was going to be given adaptations, regardless."

Lexo shook his head. "That wasn't what I meant. They are using you, torturing you, and then not giving you any relief or compassion. That is not humanity, that is the work of a parasite."

Duss glided to the edge of the tank and looked at Lexo. "I am of your bloodline, so watch your tone. You may have chosen the path of the warrior against the wishes of your family, but I chose science and research. That was what I gave my mind and body to when your grandmother was just a child. She understood, so you had better adjust your attitude."

Lexo blinked. "That... isn't likely."

Duss waved his hand through the air. "We brought you here for two purposes. The first is to pilot this vessel, the second is as a companion to our conduit. You are right, and we did what was right at the time. Now it is time to do something else."

Alphy checked the records she had access to. Duss Merker had been a researcher who devoted his life to the nanite sciences. His family was still around today, and Stephanie and Lexo were listed among his descendants. It was annoying to have to hunt for information, but while she had access to all the data generated by humankind, she had to know what she was looking for before she could find it.

She leaned her elbows on the railing and looked them in the eyes, one at a time. "What do you mean *conduit*?"

Trell looked to the others, and their

minds went silent inside hers.

She looked to Lexo. "They aren't answering."

He was staring at Duss's projection and didn't answer her.

She snorted and slapped her hand against the railing. "Guys! Answer. Conduit to what?"

Onic focused on her, "Conduit to the ship. We had this ship built with a number of capabilities, but we were incompatible with the equipment. We can reach to the stars via our satellites, but we can't steer the damned ship."

Alphy laughed. "Neither could I. The controls were all dead ends."

"And yet you got us moving." Duss had a smile on his features.

Alphy didn't have a response to that except to say, "You didn't want me to get the ship in motion."

Trell chuckled. "Of course, we did. We just didn't want to make it easy."

Onic waved his hand. "It wasn't like that. It was your hands that would have to do the work. Our voices would have simply distracted you from your purpose."

Lexo cleared his throat. "You can hear them?"

Alphy snorted. "All the time. The data runs through me, but they pull it in."

"So, this evening..."

She wrinkled her nose. "I reset to keep from burning out. I went through the first eight months fine, but then, I shorted out. They did the only thing they could think of. They reset my systems... all of them. After that, it became regular maintenance of my systems."

Lexo stared before he let out a snort. "They turned you off and on again?"

"Yup." She gripped the railing again. "I just wish they would give me a heads-up before they do it. Those few moments trapped in my body before my motor control comes back online are agony. It is just like the moment after the explosion when I couldn't move and everything burned with pain."

The boys went silent.

"You remember it?"

"Yeah. I do. I think Lucky is the only one who might have memory loss. She got the blast full frontal." She looked over at Lexo. "If they are willing to talk to you in this form, I can leave you to it. I have to get back to my attempts to sleep, or I will short out when I need to focus."

She patted her physical companion on the arm and left him to the weird mercies of the Triad.

* * * *

When the last flutter of the robe disappeared, Lexo turned back to the brains encased in nanites.

"What was done to her?"

Trell straightened. "That is classified."

Duss huffed and looked toward his descendant. "The Splice were attempting to alter a human to use them for communications. The other human was successful and was used to feed the Splice misinformation about troop movements, as well as gain superior technology. Aria had the channels opened, but there was no fine tuning. She can snag input from any source, analyze and store it without thinking."

"The Splice did that to her?"

Duss nodded. "They opened the pathways, but it was the Splice changes that allowed us to make use of that alteration."

Lexo scowled. "What were you doing for communication before that?"

"We would summon support vehicles, and we had the system programmed for maintenance. It was a quiet but safe existence."

"What changed?"

The Triad looked to each other before Trell said, "Humanity began to consume itself from within. With the bulk of the threat of the Splice eliminated, folk chafed at the martial law that had been set in place. They demanded their rights, and a movement to communicate with the Splice began. The shield was nearly complete, so Earth reduced the armed forces that they were sending to the war effort. They faded the lives of those who died into the regretful past."

"I read about the shield. Do you think it will hold?"

Onic snorted. "Like hell. One Splice warship in a direct assault and it would short out in seconds. They may as well be hiding behind a curtain."

Lexo scowled. "Why do they think it will hold?"

"Because the information they got from the Splice communicator tells them it will. It's a bait that the Splice have used through dozens of worlds. They give them the hope of protection and then wait until the defending forces are withdrawn. At that point, they strike."

Lexo tightened his hands on the railing. "What can we do?"

"You can fly, we can plan. Gathering our forces is our primary concern. Once they are on this vessel, we will prepare for our counteroffensive."

"What is the purpose of the offensive?"

"Genocide of the Splice." The Triad's voices blended together on their announcement of purpose.

"Right. What is Alphy's purpose?"

Duss smiled. "She is our conduit. She is the master of this vessel. She will make it all it can be when the time is right. Aria is essential."

Lexo raised his brows, "Did anyone tell Alphy that she is in charge?"

The Triad looked at each other, and they swiftly disappeared back below the swirling liquid nanites.

Apparently, the conversation was over. Lexo looked around one more time, and then, he returned to his quarters with only a short detour to check on Alphy.

Her even breathing and look of innocence identified her as in a deep sleep. Lexo watched her for a few minutes and then he headed to his room.

He had no idea what Alphy would feel like in the morning, but if her body had been reset, she would probably be hung over. He would be.

Chapter Seven

*A*lphy moved around the dining hall, humming softly as she got her breakfast just the way she liked it.

She had just settled in to eat when Lexo appeared, looking as if he had been riding outside the ship instead of inside. "Morning, Lexo."

"Um, morning, Alphy. You look... great."

She chuckled. "I always do after a reset. All my nanites got jump started into action. Sorry, you had to come to my rescue."

"It was my pleasure. I learned a lot about this vessel that makes the unusual wiring make sense."

Alphy blinked. "The Triad talked to you?"

"No, I rested for an hour, explored the systems for three, and then, got another hour of rest."

"Right. Well, did you learn anything useful?"

"I believe so." As he spoke, he got his meal and grabbed a mug of the fresh coffee.

He settled in across from her, and she kept eating while he got started.

"Well, what did you learn?" She paused to nibble at a strip of bacon.

"I learned that this vessel isn't an asteroid or a space station. It is something else, but the configuration doesn't make sense."

Alphy chuckled. "Welcome to my world. Everything is just slightly off."

Lexo devoured his meal and took care of his tray, returning with another cup of coffee. "So, what are my duties as your companion?"

His expression was impish as he sipped at the steaming dark brew.

She sighed. "I don't know. You are my best friend's brother, so I think you are off limits for any shenanigans."

He shook his head. "Nope. I am the older brother, not the younger. I am definitely in the shenanigan category."

Alphy blushed. "Ah. I see. You are declaring your eligibility?"

"Definitely. I also want to convince you of my suitability before we get to the base."

She blinked. "Before there are other candidates for my hand?"

"Or any other body part. I believe that we would be good together."

Alphy stared at him. "I don't even know you."

"That is incorrect. You have my file, you know my sister. What else is there to know?"

She blinked. "Um... I don't know. There just seems like there should be more. Shouldn't there?"

He was about to answer when an alarm sounded.

Alphy stood and ran for the bridge.

Lexo kept pace with her. "What is that alarm?"

"Proximity warning. There is a Splice ship out there."

The guys were feeding her information from distant relay stations. They were panicked about the incursion. Apparently, having a Splice ship discover them while they chugged through the stars wasn't part of their plan.

"How do you know it isn't just a stellar event?"

Lexo could carry on a normal conversation while he ran. Good breath control. She would have to keep that in mind.

"This ship can and has taken direct

meteor strikes. That is what it is built for. If someone is heading toward us, they are doing it in a straight line and without any gravitational curves. They are aiming for us."

He nodded. "Right. Where are the weapons?"

She snorted. "There are handheld weapons only. I am just heading to the command deck to arm the interior systems. If they catch us, they are coming aboard."

"Do I have access to the weapons' vault?"

"I never closed the door, so I will say yes."

He grunted and passed her on the way to the deck.

By the time she got to the deck, he was gone, so she grabbed a few guns, a belt, and a backup charge pack and headed over to the cradle.

She would have used the array on the

command deck, but Lexo had torn it apart during his renovations.

She set the weapons to the side of the cradle and breathed deeply to put her into a receptive state. The guys were with her as she sent her senses into the stars.

The satellites told her the same story over and over. There was only one ship nearby, and based on its speed, it would be latching onto their ship in the next ten minutes. The big question was where would the entry point be.

The interior systems of the ship were armed for any non-human or nanite tissue. Lexo should be fine.

Remain with us. You require protection.

Alphy blinked and sat up. "No. Lexo is not my protector, he is my pilot. I am not going to leave him out there to defend me."

We need you.

"I don't care, and I don't plan on dying. I need to defend what has become my home." She got out of the cradle and strapped on the guns. She was much more comfortable with pistol-style weapons than the long-range rifles.

"Guys, I will ask you one thing. Please let me know where they are coming in when they get here."

There was silence before the chorus of, *We will.*

She exhaled slowly and went to stage for defense near the shuttle bay. She was almost hoping that the Splice ran into Lexo first, seeing the patchwork aliens again was not something she had ever imagined. It was a bit cowardly, but she was practical. Surviving the Splice one time was unlikely. Twice would be impossible.

She locked her senses to the station, opened the link between her and the Triad wide, and she waited.

They are coming in through exhaust vent thirty-seven. There are only three of them, and their ship is attached to the hull.

She closed her eyes for a moment and nodded when she opened them, taking off at a run and heading toward the oxygen farm. The vent was only opened in emergencies. If the umbilical to their ship was lost, the plants would be in danger. That was definitely something that Alphy was willing to act on. She liked breathing. It was a hard habit to break.

The fans blew the scent of the Splice to her before she saw them. The musky mix of a dozen species was unmistakable. If they hadn't been assembled in a horrific patchwork, it might have even been an intriguing mix.

Her stomach churned, and she got her weapons ready. The Splice didn't speak. They communicated on a frequency that no human could hear, but it was effective. She listened for the slight scuff of boots approaching down the hall near her ambush point. When she heard that slight signal, she swung into the open expanse, sighted, and fired.

The first Splice was a walking horror. She shot it in the shoulder, the chest, the neck, and the thigh. It collapsed without a sound.

She dodged behind her corner as the other two fought back.

The sound of the stun pulse sent a chill down her spine. It set off a cascade of memories that slowed her as she ran for better cover.

The steady pounding of boots behind her got closer as she approached her goal. When she skidded around the corner, she fell to the floor, but the searing crackle of burned Splice was worth the road rash.

She got to her feet and bolted for cover. The third member of the party wouldn't be as stupid as the other two. The footfalls behind her were more cautious now but no less relentless.

When a bolt shot past her and to the defense node, her hope sank. She had been counting on the Splice to pursue her into one of the death alleys that were dotted around the vessel, but it seemed that he had caught on to what delivered the charge.

She focused on running, and when a figure stepped out in front of her, she hit the deck and slid past it as Lexo lifted his rifle and blasted the Splice.

"Is that the last one?"

She lay face down on the decking and grunted. "Yes."

"Is their ship still attached?"

Alphy pushed herself up. "Yes. It is in a sensitive place, so it has to be detached with care."

"I can do that. Do we have a disposal for the bodies?"

She shuddered. "No. We need to get them onto their ship and dump it."

"Dump it?"

"Set it on course and launch it into a star or something."

Lexo helped her to her feet. "Do you know of one conveniently located?"

She grimaced. "No. But I can find one."

"Can you read Splice? I haven't flown one of their vessels before, so I don't know if they have autopilot."

Alphy shuddered. "I can find out. Can you handle the bodies?"

"Yeah. Not the best way to start the day, but yeah."

She shuddered again and stiffened her shoulders. "Good. Let's go."

A maintenance bot pulled up with a stack of bags on it.

Alphy swallowed slowly and grabbed

the top bag. "I am guessing that the guys want us to bag them up for transport."

"Can't you ask them?"

She shook her head. "Nope. They shut off when I am freaking out or ill. Right now, I am both. I really hate these things."

"They are conscious, thinking be-ings." It was amazing that he could be so analytical as he took the bag from her and flipped it out next to the corpse.

"Who are trying to hunt humanity to extinction."

"Right." He grunted as he grabbed the Splice and rolled it into the bag. There was a dark bloodstain on the decking, but the small army of maintenance bots was standing by to do their work.

It was only when the bag was closed and the Splice was hidden that Alphy realized she was clutching herself. She was literally holding herself together.

She went to a panel and summoned a

carrier. It seemed easier than hauling corpses through the ship.

"The carrier will be here in a moment."

Lexo nodded and settled his weapon comfortably at his hip. "You took out two of them on your own."

She grimaced. "You could call it that."

"Are they dead?"

Alphy nodded. "Oh, yeah."

He nodded. "Good. Any chance of any more?"

"The guys said there were only three, and I trust their access to the scanners."

The transport platform arrived, and she helped Lexo heave the body onto it. She gagged and straightened, grabbing the two folded bags from the maintenance bot before leading the way to her second victim.

"He's this way."

Lexo shook his head as he kept step with her. "You really are repulsed by them."

"Oh, yeah. Just an image makes my skin crawl."

He blinked. "Is this a long-standing issue?"

She kept walking. "Just since they carved up my entire workgroup piece by piece. Seeing them coming and wondering if I was next was only second to the horror of seeing those taken coming back in pieces. If they came back at all."

He didn't say anything, just moved slightly closer to her.

They walked the halls and finally found the second body. It was still smoking.

"Huh, I ran faster and farther than I thought." Alphy looked at the Splice who had run into the defense system.

"What the hell did that?"

She quirked her lips to hide the bile that was rising. "My rapier wit. Bag him up."

Lexo started to move the corpse, and he paused to look over his shoulder at her. "Huh, this is an interesting first date."

"Whoa. Date?"

"Well, we have been brought together by the Triad. I thought that we should date before anything else happens. This is a weird couple's activity, but I am willing to work on expunging the Splice with you."

Well, she was so speechless that her shock drove out her distaste at the thought of the Splice. That was new.

Chapter Eight

$\mathcal{T}$he Splice ship was mercifully empty. Alphy hummed to herself as she read the controls. She paused and said, "I think I have it. You enter coordinates here, set propulsion here, and then, the ship will go through its detachment sequence."

Lexo was watching over her shoulder. "That's it?"

"Yup. It is very point-and-shoot."

Alphy rubbed her hands together and looked at the small cockpit of the scouting vessel. "Right. We should be able to launch this sucker by delayed response, or at least a remote."

"Do you have a remote?"

She shook her head. "No, but the guys are good at this kinda thing. I am pretty sure that the fabricators are already assembling what we need."

They are. The bots will be delivering it in five minutes. Please, link with the Splice ship for data absorption. Duss's words were calm, but they were an order.

Alphy looked to Lexo. "The control unit will be here in five minutes. In the meantime, I have to get to work."

"What?"

"I need to scour the systems for information. I just wanted to give you a head's up in case you wondered."

Lexo put his hand on her shoulder. "Is that safe?"

She chuckled. "Definitely not. Here I go."

She pressed her fingers to the active screen, and her nanites filled the system.

The alien information flowed through

her and into the Triad. Alphy remained still as her nanites retrieved all they could and then returned to her in a rush.

She gasped and staggered back. "Right. Got it. Is the remote here yet?"

Lexo straightened from his position next to her. He held her steady while she fought for balance. "I installed it an hour ago. What were you doing?"

She blinked slowly as the real world took up its place around her. "I was working. Data sorting."

"How? Your fingers didn't move."

She sighed. "Can we discuss this over lunch? It has been a very trying day."

"Right. Of course. Sure. Come with me."

Alphy smirked as he led her back to her home. It was as if he was the senior staff and not just the pilot, or she was an invalid. Either way, it was not flattering.

"I know the way home, Lexo. You don't have to hold me up."

They walked through the narrow halls of the Splice ship, breathing as shallowly as possible. The stench of fear mingled with the alien musks produced a smell so strong she could taste it. She knew that smell. She had spent time in that smell.

Alphy bolted for the hatch that connected the Splice ship to her station. The moment she was safe, she doubled over and dry heaved onto the deck.

"Are you all right?"

She waved at him and croaked, "Get that thing out of here."

"Right. Sealing the breach." Lexo slammed a sheet of metal against the hole in the hull that had been carved by the incursion.

She shivered and leaned against the wall as the maintenance bots whirred and welded the hole closed.

When the seal was confirmed, Lexo went to the nearest control panel and keyed in a series of commands. "Do you have the coordinates?"

She nodded and stood next to him, typing as quickly as she could. "That should do it. It is on the other side of this station, so aside from the slight pause, there should be no indication that they found anything at this position."

"Why is that important?"

She smiled slightly, "Because they didn't report finding us, and their ships are all interlinked. That is how they can attack entire planets once they are sure of compatibility."

The flood of information in her mind had left pools of data that her conscious thoughts could access. She saw species with wings, tails, and other adaptations that the Splice wanted. Humans were just filler for the special bits and pieces that they wanted to hold together, and as such, they were valuable. She knew that already. She had been on the front-lines of the first harvest.

The hiss of the umbilical releasing was a relief. The ship would float a safe distance away, and then, the engines would fire.

"It is set to go. Are there satellites that can monitor it?"

Alphy nodded. "Yup. The guys are on it."

"Are they speaking to you now?"

"Not in a manner that counts as speech. I get flickers from the direct feed of the ship's satellites." She started to head for the dining hall when he grabbed her arm.

"Are you sure you are all right?"

She paused and linked her arm with his. "I will be fine after I scrub my hands, eat, and then go for a swim in the oxygen farm."

He brightened. "Swim?"

"Yup. There is a freshwater tank embedded in the floor. It is almost like a lake."

They walked in step down the hall, the dried blood of the Splice still on their skin. The sonic scrubber was waiting for them, and Alphy stuck her hands in the machine near the door of the dining hall.

When it was Lexo's turn, he admitted, "That is a handy thing."

"It is. I am pretty sure it was a tech with small kids that put it in all the mess halls of the Earth forces."

"It seems likely."

With their hands and forearms clean, it was time to get something to eat. A scan of her palm resulted in the ship preparing two trays for her. She took one in each hand and walked to the tables before returning to the dispenser for some coffee, water, tea, soda, and anything else that the unit could come up with. She was parched.

The tray wobbled as she walked, but

Lexo was busy with his own meal and didn't have a free hand. She set the tray down with a sigh.

Lexo eyed her selections. "That is quite the meal."

"Yup, but apparently, I need it, so I will work my way through it." She settled in and lifted her spork. She had a lot of work to do.

When she cleared the first tray, Lexo took it away for her. She continued on through the second and finally sat back with a sigh. Everything was gone, but she felt like she had eaten a light snack and not an entire buffet.

Lexo was staring at her, his chin resting on his hands, his elbows on the table. "Wow. That was hot."

She looked at him and grinned. "You have strange tastes, Lexo."

He shrugged. "I have been away from home a long time. A woman with an appetite is the most encouraging thing I have seen recently."

She stretched, thrusting her arms upward, pulling at the muscles of her shoulders. "Right. Now a swim."

He chuckled and blinked. "Well, now that stretch is the most encouraging thing I have seen. Aren't you supposed to wait at least an hour after eating before you swim?"

Alphy smirked and took care of her final dishes. "That is an old wives' tale, and it only applies to wearing a suit."

Lexo was on his feet in an instant. "Lead the way."

The interior arboretum was gorgeous, as always.

"Why would the Triad have this installed on their vessel?"

Alphy stripped. "I neither know nor care. All I know is that it feels almost like I am back on Earth. It makes me feel like I am home."

The ceiling above was fifteen stories away. The huge central spoke housed the trees and the lake that was central to the water-processing and oxygen systems.

She didn't look at her companion, just waded into the lake and started to swim. The splash behind her spoke volumes.

She turned, and he was gone.

Shrugging, she continued to swim back and forth, occasionally seeing his head above the surface as he cruised around the open water.

She was floating on her back and sculling slowly through the water when he appeared at her side.

"You really do like the water." He swam next to her as she slipped slowly across the surface.

"I really do. You seem to be having fun as well."

He grinned. "I am. I confess I wasn't sure I could swim with the adaptations, but they don't hold me back."

"If you didn't get a shower warning, they wouldn't be a problem. Hell, your family perfected this technology. You should know that water isn't an issue." She smiled and kept looking up at the distant ceiling.

"Knowing it and testing it are two different issues."

Alphy chuckled. "Yeah, it took me six months to work up the nerve to go for a swim. Once I managed it, I never looked back."

He floated next to her. "It is a pity that you can't see the stars."

She sighed. "And a little weird. This entire area is domed in."

She let her legs drop and treaded water beside him. "So, how much retrofitting did Stitch give you?"

He snorted and matched her position. "She went over all the empty weapons casings and set me up with some new personal defense systems."

"Why didn't you use them against the Splice?"

He blinked and smiled. "Because I had a gun?"

She laughed. "Right. I forgot about that."

"The defense system is only good twenty feet and closer. I don't like the Splice getting that close."

They were less than two feet from each other, the water around them was crystal clear, and she could see every inch of him below the rippling surface.

"You were badly damaged."

He quirked his lips. "Not flattering but accurate."

"How?"

"Not all at once. A crushing impact ship to ship, an explosion on board. And the injury that started it all, a vehicular accident back on Earth." He shrugged.

"So, that is where they injected you

with nanites to begin with. Did they make you want to join the fight?"

"No. Seeing humanity at risk, knowing how vulnerable we were to alien attack, and knowing that I loved to fly sent me to the stars."

"Despite what your family wanted."

He smiled. "Only Stephanie supported my decision to join the defense force. She even joked that she would join as well. That didn't go over well with our parents, but I am guessing she eventually got herself up and into action."

"Yeah, they did an all-call for any women with analytical, engineering, or medical skills. They set up the Adaptation Base to remake stronger and better-balanced cyborgs. Your sister is amazing with her knowledge of the way the human body works."

He nodded. "She was always good at biological analysis. It was her suggestion to take the nanites out of the lab and put them into my body. My response time got faster, vision got better, and my skin was aware of every breath of air that crossed it."

"In that case, being wounded must have sucked."

Lexo laughed, "You have no idea."

Alphy lifted her hand and sighed. "Well, I am just about to get pruney, so I am heading back to shore."

"I will join you. Do you think that the bots will have scrubbed the ship clean by now?"

She turned and stroked toward the shore. "Positive. I am pretty sure it was clean before we finished eating."

He easily outpaced her. His arms moved more water.

Lexo was on the shore before she was, and as she waded out of the water, she could see that he appreciated the view.

"Your body is completely human except for your scalp and spine. It is a miracle that you came out of the blast with such minimal damage."

Alphy looked down at her skin, beaded with water and pebbled with a chill. "It didn't feel like minimal damage at the time."

He stepped forward to take her hands, and he said, "I know this is going to come out pervy considering our state of undress, but you are beautiful covered in grime, eating with both hands, or just as you are. Your mind is amazing, and you being able to keep your sanity under these conditions shows remarkable self-possession."

"Um. Thanks. I think you are pretty, too."

He chuckled and leaned in to kiss her.

She felt his lips press against hers, and three eager and interested minds were pressing back.

She pulled away and whispered, "I need to spend some time in the cradle. I have to give the guys something else to focus on."

He quirked his lips. "Really?"

"Unless you want to be in the middle of a five way… yes."

Chapter Nine

$\mathcal{D}$o you often wander around the ship naked?"

Alphy laughed. "Only when I forget to bring a change of clothing to the lake and what I was wearing is covered in Splice blood. This is the better alternative."

He nodded. "I agree, but it feels weird."

"You get used to it. There isn't anyone else here, and the Triad is a little on the pervy side no matter what I am wearing. This shuts them up."

"It does leave me nearly speechless."

"Nearly?" She snorted.

"Well, I need to be able to express my

admiration for your grace and poise."

"Excellent. I admire your ability to point down the path no matter which direction we are headed in."

He glanced down at his erection and shrugged. "It is very forward thinking."

Her giggled echoed through the halls.

He reached out and took her hands, and after a few steps staring at it, she settled into a gait that kept her close enough to him to feel his body heat.

It was a weird Adam and Eve moment, but Alphy was happy to surrender to the fantasy, just a little.

The surface of the cradle was cool on her skin. She had never gone into the data stream with someone watching her before, and it took her longer than usual to settle herself.

"Okay, here we go."

She opened her mind and pulled the Triad with her, opening all the satellites and gaining what intel she could.

Reports were flooding in from around the sector. Cyborg outposts were breaking away from their stations and making their way toward Stitch's base. Her call had started a slow progression of humans toward their own kind. The military was over; it was time for a new colony and a new focus in their war against the Splice.

She came out of it with a shiver. "Wow. That is a lot of action."

"What is it?"

She sat up and grinned. "Your sister is a force of nature or technology. She is calling for forces to mobilize and a new colony to be started."

"You aren't serious."

"Yeah, I am. Since all I can really do is listen to the myriad stations and broadcasts, I am deadly serious. It is all anyone is talking about on the coded channels."

"You can hear it?"

Alphy laughed. "I can hear and see it. My nanites do the translation for me. It is sort of like I am floating in a web of signals and listening to them all at once."

"Can I try it?"

She looked to the body-shaped cradle. "I don't think you would fit."

"May I try?"

No. It would be far too dangerous. His brain would blow apart.

She wrinkled her nose. "The Triad says no, or at least, Trell does."

"Does he say why?"

She got out of her station and rose to her feet. "He says your brain would explode."

"I don't think that is literal."

Alphy moved past him down the steps and headed for the nearest fabrication unit. "I am pretty sure it was. He accompanied the warning with a visual."

"Ah. What did it look like?"

She grinned as the machine whirred to produce her order. "Constipation followed by surprise."

He looked as if he wanted to discuss it further, but he settled for ordering a change of clothing.

She got her jumpsuit from the unit and stepped into it. She was sealing the closure when Lexo got his.

Her feet were happy that they were no longer in contact with the hard decking. She wiggled her toes and watched the muscles of Lexo's thighs and backside flex and twist as he got dressed. It was a pity to watch the silvered skin of his hips and ribs disappear under fabric.

The breadth of his shoulders was impressive no matter what he wore.

Alphy clawed her hair back and put it in a messy bun.

"Well, the boys are busy playing with trajectories and transmissions. If you want my undivided attention, this is literally the best time to take it."

Lexo paused with the neckline of his suit open. "In that case..."

He wrapped her in his arms and kissed her. Apparently, hesitation wasn't in his repertoire.

She closed her eyes and threaded her fingers through his hair. The strands were short, but she managed to get a grip to hold him tight.

Alphy was pulling his suit open when the proximity alarm went off again.

She wrenched away. "Shit!"

A triad of Splice ships have slipped past our defenses. There was no indicator of their approach, so we are attempting to trace their trajectories. Onic's voice was tense.

"When will they be on the hull?"

They have attached. They will be inside in minutes.

Lexo was staring at her. She swallowed slowly. "The Splice are here."

"I gathered as much. How much time do we have?"

"Enough to get to the armoury but not enough time to pull the weapons."

Lexo nodded. "Let's go."

They ran through the ship and armed themselves. On the way, she asked, "Did you want to stay together or split up?"

"Stay together. If we are the only life signs on the ship, they will converge on us. Numbers are definitely a good thing."

We are sending out a distress signal. The base is close enough to send out small ships to assist. Onic's voice was tense.

Alphy checked her rifle's sight before she armed the interior defenses.

"What is the situation?"

"Apparently, we are close enough to the base to call for help, but in the meantime, I have armed the interior defenses. They will take out any Splice who get close. Their alien parts will set off the scanner, and that triggers the energy pulse.”

“Which fries them into toast.”

“Yup.”

“How far apart are the nodes?”

“They are set at random around the ship. It is a weird configuration.”

“Are the Triad protected?”

“Oh, yeah. Nothing is getting at them. They have a physical shield that they can use, but once they do, they can’t listen in to what is going on.”

“Can you directly connect with the ship?”

Alphy nodded. “I can if I have to. It will put me out of commission while I use the interior scanners, but we can get an idea of where the Splice are.”

I will be your eyes. We have ten Splice in the ship. They appear to be searching for something. They have gathered and are moving in a group. They are passing the entertainment complex right now.

She sighed and passed Duss's information to Lexo. "They are on the way past the movie theatre. Ten Splice, moving together."

He stared at her. "Moving together? They don't do that."

"They are doing it now."

"How do you know?"

"Duss is giving me information. They are keeping their link to the ship open wide and feeding me locations."

"Will that put them in danger?"

"Probably. They are willing to stay with me until the Splice get within a hundred metres of them."

Lexo nodded. "Good. Are you ready for this?"

"No, but I am a relatively good shot."

He cocked his head. "Is there a better place to wait for them?"

"Sure. I have just the spot."

She kept the position of the approaching intruders in her mind and led Lexo back the way they had come and up onto a catwalk overlooking the hallway. They had one hundred eighty degrees of vision, and no one could approach from underneath without their seeing it. The hub of connecting tunnels opened into a wide atrium that went up to the inner hull. Other catwalks were available, but none were accessible from their position. This was the best possible place.

"Wait. I will take the first shots."

She nodded and lay as flat as she could, sighting at the entry point where the Splice would emerge.

Seconds dragged into minutes, and the first light scuff of a foot snapped her into alertness. She rolled to her back and took aim at where her senses told her to shoot.

The grunting hiss and bloody thud

next to her were proof that she wasn't insane. The rush of bodies was heard rather than seen. The fuckers were invisible.

"Back to back," Lexo growled it as the lack of a visible enemy hampered their chance to aim.

She felt the heavy wall of him against her back, and she kept firing until the power cartridge was empty. Two corpses were stacked in front of her as she pulled her secondary weapons, but when hands grabbed her, and the crackle of a stun blast hit her, she dropped them.

Her body was numb, and she knew that her mind would shut down next, but that wasn't what happened. She was pinned to one of the creatures, and they were hauling her away.

Instead of passing out as the Splice carried her away from the still-embattled Lexo, her hands flexed and her body flared back into awareness.

She gathered her strength, gripped the arm around her waist, and squeezed with all her might. The sound of the bone splintering shocked her, but her captor dropped her immediately.

Alphy scuttled backward until her spine was pressed against the wall. If she concentrated, she could see the faint outline of the Splice who was approaching her. She kicked outward and upward with all her strength. Tissue shredded and he staggered back.

The crackle and twist of light pulled him away from her, and another lashing of energy tore him in two.

Alphy turned her head, and Lexo stood, covered in blood with whips emerging from the palms of his hands.

The crackle sounded again, and the one who had grabbed her was gripped and torn in two, his head severed neatly from his body.

Alphy stared at the head as it went

from translucent to opaque. She shuddered at the shock and horror in the dead eyes.

The light scuttling of another invader brought her back to her predicament. She clenched her fist and took aim but staggered forward as the whips tore the last Splice apart.

"Duss, did we get them all?"

All alien life signs are fading. When you are finished with cleanup, come to the tank. It is time to get this ship into its proper configuration.

She didn't ask what he was talking about. It wasn't her main concern. "Keep one to test it, Lexo. The camo is new, and I need to know how they are doing it."

"Right. Any preference?"

"One of the ones that we shot. Something in one piece."

Lexo nodded, and the whips retracted into his hands. "Got it. I will set one aside. Where is the medical facility?”

“Next to the gym.”

“I will get on that if you start with the body bags.”

She wrinkled her nose. “Right. The bots are on the way.”

“Great. I will find a whole one, you grab some heads.” He smiled tersely and headed for their previous hiding place that hadn’t done any good at all.

Alphy looked at the bot bringing the body bags to her. “Do you know which head goes with which body?”

The bot remained silent.

“Right. I thought so. Well, at least he carved them into manageable chunks.”

She got to work, grabbing slick and bloody parts and stuffing them into the bags. “Why is it that the ladies always get stuck with the cleanup?”

The bot still didn’t answer.

Chapter Ten

So, there is a theatre?" Lexo smiled at her as the last of the bodies were dumped into space, their empty vessels still attached to the ship.

"Yup. This was a fully kitted-out facility, which is funny considering the guys can't do anything." She tried wiping the blood off on her suit, but there wasn't a clean spot to work with.

"It is a little odd. So, do you want to clean up now or deal with the ships?"

Leave the ships. We are dealing with the signals. Onic's voice was grim.

"They say to leave the ships. They are dealing with them."

Lexo shrugged. "Right. Well, I think a

shower is in order."

"You and me both."

"I was offering you the use of my shower and sharing water to conserve resources."

Alphy blinked. "Wow. That is... sure. To your quarters then."

He grinned, and they walked through the halls, leaving bloody footprints all the way to the crew quarters.

Peeling off the suits was a relief that both of them expressed the moment that they hit the floor. "Ahhh."

Alphy grinned and turned on his shower, stepping inside when the temperature was where she liked it.

The blood was sticky, and it grudgingly rinsed off.

"Turn around, and I will help you get your back." Lexo was in the shower next to her, and a large, foamy scrubber accompanied his offer.

She nodded and turned her back,

working at her breasts and belly to get herself as clean as possible with her own hands while her hair dripped with diluted gore.

When she was clean, she returned the favour, scrubbing the muscular mix of man and nanites until all the places she was willing to reach were clean. He grinned and took care of the rest.

Wrapped in towels, they left the bathroom, and he gestured to his couch. "Care to sit? I believe we have a few things to discuss."

She grimaced and took up a perch on his couch. "So, what do you want to discuss?"

"Well, you seem to react very calmly to the energy whips I used."

Alphy shrugged. "You did mention that you had defensive weapons. I assume that that is what those were."

"Yes. Stephanie had them installed. I hadn't used them yet."

"Well, you looked like a natural."

He smiled slightly. "Thanks. It felt very natural, but I guess, that is what my sister does."

Alphy smiled slightly. "She is good at it."

"Right, now, what exactly are your adaptations?"

She frowned. "I told you, some brain and spinal alterations. That is all that is in my file."

"You definitely have had other replacements done. I don't know of anyone who could crush a Splice with their bare hands."

Alphy looked down at her hands, and they looked like her hands. There was no silvery tissue to let her know that she was a cyborg, but then, she hadn't really had a medical check in the last three years. "I think I need to go to medical."

Three voices in her mind screamed, *No!*

She clutched her skull as they continued to shout that she was fine, she didn't need a check, she should not use the scanners.

Lexo was at her side, his hand on her knee. "What is it?"

"The Triad would like me to not go to the med centre. They are saying that you are insane and that I am fine."

He gave her a sober look. "Do you believe them?"

"No, but I can also feel their worry for me."

Lexo sighed. "Do you want to know what actually happened to you?"

She thought about it before she nodded. "I think so. I am guessing I am ready to face whatever actually happened, now."

"Was there ever any doubt?"

"Of course. A sense of revulsion ran through me every time I thought about checking up on what implants are actually in my body." She wrinkled her nose. "It was probably a subroutine to keep me from looking."

"Likely. Now, do you want to get dressed, or is wandering around naked on the table again?"

Alphy laughed and got to her feet. "I will be right back. Find some pants."

She checked to make sure that her towel was in place and walked over to her room. Alphy left the door open as she dropped the towel and went in search of clothing. She could almost feel Lexo's attentive gaze on her, but she wasn't going to check to see if he was looking. She just assumed that he was.

The suit that she put on was her favourite, and it would be scanner friendly.

The more she thought about the scans, the queasier she became. Since the Splice were being cleaned up around the ship, there was no reason for the nausea.

When she had been on Adaptation Base, it had been standard to be scanned every three months. She hadn't had a scan since she arrived on this vessel. That should have been a huge clue that something wasn't quite right. Her being able to crush the Splice was just a confirming factoid. No one who didn't have implants should have been able to do any damage to the armoured limbs of the aliens. That meant that there was more going on under her skin than she was aware of. The only way to find out what was going on was to make her way to medical.

She gagged and put her hair up in a ponytail before heading to the hall.

Lexo was leaning against the wall outside his door, and he smiled. "Ready?"

"Yup, but I warn you, I may puke or faint. I really don't want to go, but I want to go if you know what I mean."

He nodded. "I do. I will make sure that you get into the scanner."

"Good. I don't know what is going to happen, but I figure you should be prepared for anything."

Lexo chuckled, and they started walking toward the med centre.

Alphy felt sick then spots swam in front of her eyes and then everything went dark.

The hum of machines was all around her when her senses returned to her.

The scanner was working her over, and she could make out the shadow of Lexo on the other side of medical.

The sense of the Triad was with her, but they weren't talking, they were waiting.

The scanner finished its final pass, and the mechanism swung aside to let her out.

Lexo was seated in a repair station, and he smiled at her from a bruised face. "I managed to get you here."

"What happened?"

"I am guessing that an automatic protocol kicked in. You fought with more strength and dexterity than I imagined you possessed. I confess to being envious of your alteration, though not that enthusiastic about the autopilot."

Alphy tried to access the Triad to get a view of the internal scans, but they weren't talking to her yet.

She went into first aid mode and got a nanite stimulator for Lexo. It would help supplement the work his nanites were already doing.

The shot had to go into tissue, so she pressed the injector to the side of his neck, and it hissed as its payload entered his system.

"I am so sorry. I didn't..."

"It is fine. Your eyes went silver, and

it was obvious that you were not driving."

She blinked. "Something took me over?"

"Check your scans. I think they explain it."

Alphy turned and headed to the readout. The displayed result was impossible.

"That can't be right."

Lexo flexed his arm and got to his feet. "It does explain your situation, but in all my family's research, this extensive an adaptation hasn't been seen. That you are moving around is a miracle."

Alphy started at the display. It was there if she was willing to accept it. She was the most extreme cyborg that she had ever heard of. The only parts of her that were natural human tissue were her brain and spinal column. Everything that housed the brain and spine was made of nanites.

She looked at her hands and focused on her skin. Her vision sharpened, and she could actually see the mechanical micro-bots that made up her body.

Alphy curled her hand into a fist. "I am not human."

Lexo put his hand on her arm. "You are as human as I am."

She looked up at him. "I beg to differ. You are only forty percent nanite and implant. I am a metal skeleton with delusions of humanity."

He pulled her to him and held her.

"You can feel my arms around you; your brain processes the information just like your body did. We don't know why you are such a massive adaptation, but the Triad has to have the information somewhere."

She could feel his heart beat in his chest and the hum of his blood as it rushed through his veins, accompanied by the nanites that were fixing the damage she had done.

"I am sorry." She mumbled it against his chest, slightly appalled at the amount of information she could get from him if she just let her senses out to play.

"It is fine. You are just a little more highly tuned than you thought. I am curious to find out how you are keeping yourself together and how the Triad got you here."

She rubbed her head against the front of his suit. "You and me both. They currently are not speaking to me."

"I believe that they are afraid of how you would react. It can't be a comfortable realization."

"It really isn't. Why aren't you freaking out? I am a woman made of nanites."

He chuckled. "My family designed them, and your brain is all you. A human is more than the body it wears; it is the mind, the soul, and the consciousness of society that creates a human. You are still you, Aria, no matter what your body is composed of."

"Thanks. It is nice that you were willing to haul me in here."

Lexo sighed and stroked her back. "I will think of a way that you can make it up to me later."

Her laugh startled her. "Thanks again. I will think of something suitable. Now, do we want to confront the sullen three?"

"You go ahead. I am going to head to the command deck and make sure we are still on course."

She stood in his embrace for a few more minutes. The warmth of his body relaxed her, and the silence helped her formulate a plan.

The Triad wanted them there for some kind of transformation, but she wanted answers first.

First and foremost, she wanted to know why the Splice had targeted her. Their behaviour had gone against everything that she knew about them. It should have been both of the humans or attack to destroy. Anything else was outside of the observed behaviours.

Shit was getting freaky.

Chapter Eleven

The cradle was the most efficient way to communicate with the brains, so Alphy settled into place and sent her mind out to have a deep and meaningful discussion of why she was a brain in a housing.

Duss's voice was the first to speak. *You are fine?*

She sighed silently, but her body probably huffed. "Of course, I am fine. I am alive, and I am conscious, most of the time. Why would you think otherwise?"

Most of those who have had a transplant of your type have gone insane within days of knowing what they were. Onic's voice was grim.

"I am not most people. I am a survivor by nature."

Humans do not survive what happened to you. You were a statistical anomaly, and as such, came to our attention immediately.

Trell's voice came to her. *Would you like to see the original surveillance footage? You will understand what happened a little better if you see it.*

She would have cocked her head if she was physically with them. "I have seen the footage."

You have not seen it all. Your friends came to your aid as quickly as they could, but they were injured, and there was nothing that could be done.

Alphy steeled herself to relive the explosion. "Go ahead."

They didn't hesitate, and she was soon looking through the security camera over the joyous party filled with women and laughter... and then it exploded.

Alphy watched herself being thrown up and against the wall by the blast. The way she dropped to the floor wasn't good. It wasn't a dropped doll; it was like watching a bag of pudding knocked off a table.

Endless seconds ticked by as the women gathered themselves. A few were already gone. The lifeless bodies were unmistakable.

When the medics charged in, they bypassed Alphy as one of the dead, but then one of them paused and turned to her. "Shit! She's alive!"

They eased her onto a gurney, and one whisked her out of the party area and down toward medical.

Alphy watched the rest of her friends receive assistance or be covered for later transport, and then, she switched her view to the body in medical.

Lucky had gotten the worst of the blast, face and hands had been ravaged, but she still reached out and whispered to her medic, pointing at Alphy.

This was where your friends ordered you to be put in stasis for later repair. While you slept, the medics did what they could, but you were shattered. The blast wave crushed you, leaving only your brain and spine intact. The shape of the charge had been such that you ended up with the most damage of any of the survivors.

The footage whirled through a rapid buzzing of bodies around her. Lucky with two silver hands and a face to match was doing a lot of work at Alphy's bedside. Cracker pushed herself along in a wheelchair and read to Alphy while she slept.

Finally, the image of the two holding each other as they sobbed was the last on that ship as Alphy's stasis chamber was removed and settled in a shuttle.

The station that she currently resided on was the next stop. The courier loaded her into the med bay and left her, flying back to his dispatch centre.

Images of the station took over. Alphy wanted to gag, but it was fascinating as a series of nanites were poured over her body, dissolving flesh and bone. It was a smaller version of the tank that the guys floated in. She was in a tank built for one.

We are in contact with you now, linking you to the station. The process was laborious as we didn't want to alarm you or overload your system. The nanites were creating new pathways for your brain, and we tried to calm your frantic thoughts. You were in shock, panicked. You wanted to run, to fight, to find those you loved, but there was no way to do it. Eventually, after a few weeks, you were ready to join us in our tank.

She watched as the tank was transported by bots through the station with extreme care. The scene reminded her of transporting fish into a new tank.

Her tank was lowered on a sinking panel of smooth decking at the edge of the tank. A barrier was between her unit and the swirling, living metal beyond. At some unseen signal, the barrier opened, and her tank was surrounded by the maintenance nanites that took care of the Triad.

The tank disappeared, and her brain and spinal cord were gently eased into the main area of the pool.

Wait to see what happened five days later. Trell was amused.

The images went faster until there was a ripple on the surface of the pool. The ripple moved again until it was obvious that something was cruising below the silvery surface.

When a hand shot out of the pool, Alphy gasped. The silver appendage moved and grabbed the edge of the large tank. Another hand reached out and pulled on the barrier's edge.

Alphy watched herself emerge, silver skin and completely dry. The face that she knew so well frowned as it looked at her skin. The silver faded to her normal yellow-pink. Her hair flowed to her standard length, and her eyes took on their golden-brown hue. She was normal and naked.

"I remember that. You said that I wandered away from medical."

You sort of did. You reprogrammed your nanites to build you a body, and that is what they are doing. You don't need to eat, but you do. Every item that you consume is broken down and used to slowly build a new body from the inside out. In ten years, you will be half organic once again, if you wish to be.

Onic's tone was calm.

"So, what you are saying is I am more machine than woman right now, and that my body didn't survive the blast."

Duss added his sober observation. *You were pulverized. Your bones were jelly, and your circulatory system was ineffective. Left unaided, you would have been dead in hours or even minutes. Your friends saved you and provided you with the nanites that kept you from degrading into nothing. I am guessing that the programming your friend added to your systems assisted in your rise from the pool.*

Alphy felt herself smile, "With the right nanites, Lucky could program the devil himself."

I would like her to visit here one day. Perhaps we could all share in your skill at gathering and reprogramming nanites as bodies. Onic chuckled.

"I am pretty sure she would love to

check out your data points; however, I still need to know why the Splice came to visit. They seemed to be tracking me."

I believe that your communication, coded though it was, led them here via the signal. They weren't following the information; they were following the data. Trell was grim.

"It makes sense, but it doesn't feel right. It was almost as if they were looking for me."

Onic agreed. *Perhaps they were. The Splice that initially captured you might have put you on a watch list after they altered you. They didn't send any signals after they landed, but on reviewing the video, they knew you when they saw you. They wanted to bring you in alive.*

She grinned and dug her fingers into the edge of the cradle. "Knowing what I know now, they are not going to get nearly as far as they did if they try it again. I can and will defend myself to the fullest extent, and now that I know I am not human... I don't need to act that way."

There was no response from the Triad. She chuckled. "Now, what are we going to do to the ship?"

In her mind, the three brains in the nanite fluid told her what they needed her to do, and now, she could actually do it with a bit of enjoyment.

"So, Lexo, how is the ship?"

He looked up from a monitor and smiled. "We are on trajectory. How are you feeling?"

She laughed, walking up to him and giving him a quick kiss. "I am doing great. Would you like the ship to move a little faster?"

Lexo blinked. "You know how to achieve it?"

She grinned. "Come with me. You need to get somewhere safe."

She linked her arm with his and pulled him out of the command centre. He came along without much resistance.

"What is about to happen?"

"Well, you know how some corridors lead to nowher, and others end in dangerous areas over empty spaces?"

"Yes."

"That is about to change, but I need to put you in a space where you will have oxygen and an unaltered configuration."

"So, this ship is going to rearrange itself." He nodded. "It makes a certain amount of sense considering the design."

"I am glad you think so. The guys gave me the final pattern, and I was always good at puzzles. This is going to take a few hours, so I got you some ration packs, water, and there is a lav available if you need it."

Lexo paused, and she stopped.

He turned her to look at him. "You

are really going to move the ship? All on your own?"

Alphy smiled at him. "This is something I can do. It is just a matter of filling the existing structure into its appropriate place. I just need to keep you safe, or Stitch would never forgive me."

Lexo scowled. "Are you in any danger?"

"No. You will be able to see as I link completely to the ship. It should be quite a show."

"No matter what they ask you to do, be safe first and foremost." Lexo leaned down and kissed her softly.

She sighed against his mouth and leaned into him. With all her senses, she recorded this moment—when he knew what she was and he wanted her anyway. There was no better aphrodisiac in the universe.

* * * *

Lexo watched from the sidelines as Alphy stepped into position near her cradle. Instead of lying down, a beam of light emerged from the deck beneath her feet, and she rose into the air.

The main lights of the ship went down, leaving only the glow of the emergency lighting and the brilliant pillar that Alphy danced in, and what a dance it was.

He had gone to the ballet when he was back on Earth, but this wasn't that formulaic. Her limbs moved and twisted, swayed and straightened, her position in the beam varied from ten to forty feet in the air.

Once she had shut off the power, her movements became controlled and strong. She thrust her hands, out and he heard metal move against metal in the silence of the ship.

Silence. She had shut down the engines. They were gliding on momentum alone. It wouldn't be a problem unless they got too close to a planet or other gravitational body, and he hoped that the feedback she was getting was sufficient to keep them out of trouble.

Hours went by, but he didn't look away. When the lighting came back on and the low hum of the engine coolant systems resumed, he watched her carefully.

The light around her flickered, and she descended at a more rapid pace than he liked. He ran to the dais and caught her before she collapsed to the decking.

She opened her eyes, and the silver of her irises gave way to golden brown. "You have gotta see what the ship looks like. It is fucking amazing."

He didn't have a chance to reply, his little cyborg was unconscious in his arms.

Lexo straightened and started to walk to medical when Alphy smiled brightly and leaned her head against his chest.

"Sorry about that. I had to reboot. That event took a lot of energy." She sighed. "That was definitely not in my job description."

Lexo looked down at her and kept her against him while changing his course and heading toward the command centre. "Are you sure? That was the epitome of administration if ever I saw it. You just filed a ship."

She was still giggling when they entered the bridge, and then, she laughed at the expression that must have been on his face.

Surrounding him was the most user-friendly and well-appointed captain's chair, as well as navigation, scanner stations, and weapon's command. It was every pilot's dream, and she had given it to him.

Lexo looked down at her and settled her in the captain's chair. He settled in at the navigation station and ran his hands over the controls, setting their course to resume and altering the acceleration and deceleration programs.

He glanced back at her and winked. "We will be knocking on my sister's door in twenty-one hours."

She blew him a kiss and leaned back with her eyes closed. "All satellites are stowed, and we are ready to take on additional personnel. Get us to the base so that we can justify the expense of this monster."

He grinned and activated the program. They were on their way.

Chapter Twelve

Alphy felt different. She could feel every inch of the ship like she could feel her own skin. Of course, it wasn't her own skin. Her skin had been consumed by nanites to free her brain. Weird.

The satellites were deployed once they got up to speed, and Alphy decided to warn Stitch that they were coming.

Lexo glanced at her as if he could tell she was doing something. "What are you up to?"

She chuckled. "I am making a call."

The view screen flickered, and Stitch's face filled the expanse.

Alphy grinned. "Hey, Stitch."

Stitch laughed, and tears started to run down her cheeks. "Alphy! Oh, man. You are a sight for sore eyes."

Alphy chuckled. "Right back at you. I am glad to see you in one piece."

Stitch held up one silver hand. "More or less."

"Still one piece, just with a little more tensile strength. You look great for someone who overslept."

Stitch laughed and wiped at her tears. "Yeah, well, they couldn't find the right parts for me."

"You always were a fussy fit."

"You know it. How is my brother doing? He isn't being too much of a pain in the ass, is he?"

Alphy grinned, and she shrugged. "I don't have any basis for comparison regarding his behaviour. He has been a complete gentleman the entire time."

"Damn, I was hoping you and he would hit it off."

Alphy looked over at her pilot and smirked. "We are not in a hurry. He just woke up, and I have been spending a lot of time alone. There is a time and place for everything, and rushing isn't going to do us any good."

Stitch twisted her lips. "We could all end tomorrow."

"And with our implants, we could all live for hundreds of years. It isn't something we know about, so we need to head forward at our own pace. How are your aliens?"

Stitch laughed. "Nice change of topic. They are great. They have a hive society with the queens being the power centre. I love it."

"You would."

"We can't all have *Born to be a Boss* tattooed on our asses. I will take it. It drives Niko nuts. He doesn't like it when I meet with them, but it just means he has to follow me around wherever I go. I tend to find the underground hot springs a lot."

Alphy brought up the files and put the name to the face. "Was he one of yours?"

"He was once I overhauled him. I have no idea who was responsible for assessments when I was out, but they did a shite job. The guys here have all been gone over, and they are doing great."

"I am glad to hear it."

"I can run over your adaptations if you want, see if there is anything I can tweak." Stitch looked helpful.

Alphy raised a hand. "Not necessary. I am as good as I am going to get."

As Stitch watched, Alphy let the silver nanite colour overtake her hand and face, and then, she faded back to her skin tone.

Stitch changed colour, too; she went grey. "Oh, damn, Alphy. I had no idea."

"Yeah, well, I am guessing that the actual records were altered so that no one knew what happened to me. But, I am as exceptional as I always was."

"You would have to be. Can I see your file?"

"Nope, but I will let you take a scan when we get there. Oh, we will be in orbit around your world in twenty-one hours or so. This ship is a lot faster now that it has been renovated."

"Are you secure? Do you need an escort?"

"Aw, no. We are good, Stitch. This is now a fully armed warship. If they get within five kilometres, I will blow them into Splice chunks."

"Warship? Where did you get that?" Stitch's eyes were wide.

"I found it filed under *W,* so it took me a while to get there."

They laughed, and their conversation went back to the aliens with wings and their desperation to start flying again.

"Oh, you know, I have a space that would be perfect for them. Do they want to head home?"

"Can you do that? I was going to take one of the long-range ships to their home world and try to strike a treaty. They are getting their asses kicked."

"You want a lift? I have a movie theatre and fabricators."

"How fast can you get us there? I will let them know."

Alphy grinned. "I will let you and Lexo work that out. I am just in charge of the ship, not the location. So, did you want to pick anyone else up on the way?"

Stitch chuckled. "You and I need to talk face to face. This ship is a game changer."

"You have no idea. See you tomorrow, sweetie." Alphy dismissed the call and sat back. The smile probably wouldn't leave her lips for the next two days. It was so good to be back with friends.

Lexo turned and got to his feet. "I know you probably don't need it, but let's get you a nap. You have had a helluva day."

She laughed and stood, taking his hand and walking with him through the ship and to their quarters.

He followed her into her room, and when she headed for her bed, peeling her suit off, he followed and did the same.

Naked nap was on the agenda, and she fell asleep in his arms without a care in the world.

Two hours into the nap, she roused slightly, and the guns trained on the approaching Splice ships, firing with deadly accuracy. They were torn apart by the fire of eight railguns.

Lexo ran his hand over her hip. "Is something wrong?"

She turned and faced him, snuggling against his chest and tracing the edge where flesh met nanite. "Nope. Something is very right. Do you mind waiting for sex until I can figure out how to trigger arousal? I wasn't good at it when I was human, and now, it is even more difficult."

"As long as I am the one you figure it out with, take all the time you need." He brushed his lips against her forehead then cheeks, and finally, a light kiss warmed her from the soul outward.

They clung together as the ship hurtled through the stars. It was where they belonged.

Alphy brushed at her suit and waited in the safe area outside of the shuttle bay. After some discussion, it had been decided that Stitch, Niko, and the aliens would come to the ship to see if the accommodations were suitable.

The Alguth were going to be her first true guests. She had been briefed on Commander Liakon, Sergeant Aluak, and their biologist Solouk. The other twelve reported to one of the ranking three. She wouldn't have to deal with them directly.

Through her link with the ship, she could feel the dock being pressurized. Atmosphere was populating the space, and when the door lit green, she opened it. Lexo followed her, and they approached the party who had exited the shuttle.

Alphy walked calmly for the first ten feet. After that, she squealed and ran to Stitch, hugging her tightly and whirling her around.

"I am so glad to see you, Stitch." Alphy set her on her feet.

"Ditto. I never thought that we would be having a conversation on this kind of a ship. Where did it come from?"

Alphy sighed. "Very long story. I believe introductions are in order?"

Stitch grinned. "Right. Of course. Alphy, this is Commander Liakon, Sergeant Aluak, and biologist Solouk. Oh, and this is Nikolai, my fella. Gentlemen, this is Aria Lianna Westerson-Miller Dexter. I believe you can call her Captain Dexter or Alphy if you ask her nicely. She is in charge of this ship. You have met my brother Lexo Carter. He is her pilot and navigator."

Alphy smiled at the men. "Welcome to the warship. I believe that you are all interested in a little space to stretch your wings?"

Liakon nodded and stepped forward, taking her hand and pressing a kiss to it. He widened his eyes and stared into hers for a moment. "You are extraordinary, my lady."

"Captain Dexter or Alphy. Yes, I am. Not my fault, but it is what it is. Now, if you will come with me, I can show you a space suitable for your needs while we travel." She looked to Lexo, and he offered her his arm. She settled her palm on the back of his wrist, and they got the point across to the fixated aliens.

She did a bit of a tour for Stitch's benefit. She took them past the entertainment complex, the gym, the refectory, and finally the pool and oxygen farm.

Liakon gasped, and he stepped toward her. "May we?"

She nodded. "This is why you are here. Take off."

The renovation had created a huge shatterproof dome that displayed the stars and was currently showing off the world below.

Stitch whispered, "I think I am jealous."

"Don't be. There is room for thousands on this vessel. We have enough food supplies to feed those thousands for decades. If you can bring some of those newer adaptation machines, we can take this show on the road. I wouldn't mind collecting the rest of the cyborgs and taking the fight to the Splice."

Stitch's companion stood with his mouth slightly open. "Are you serious?"

"Of course. This ship was designed to carry humanity into battle. It has waited until there were humans who could bring that into reality. That is now. I can defend us, Lexo can fly us, Stitch and yourself can refit the cyborgs and with the other survivors from our base; we can focus an attack that will make the Splice tear themselves apart to get away."

Alphy paused and watched the men with the rainbow eyes as they unfolded huge dragonfly wings and engaged in test flutters. When one of them made it off the ground, he wasted no time in rising and flying around the enormous space.

The humming of wings soon became a frenzied drone until one by one, the Alguth took off and began to do careful laps around the open area.

"Can you leave the ship?" Stitch's voice was soft.

"Yes. I am a walking pile of nanites held together by stubbornness and Lucky's programming. As long as my brain is in here, nothing can shake my cohesion. The ship can't leave without me, though. I am the centre of the systems."

"Wow. That is... different. I will take your proposal to the base. If they want to come along, I will bring them, but we will have to leave a skeleton crew behind to keep an eye on the rest of the sleepers. I don't have the resources to wake them up, but I don't want to leave them alone."

"I understand. I will make sure that I leave a monitoring satellite to make doubly sure. I understand vulnerability a lot better than I ever imagined I could." Even when she had been in the clutches of the Splice, part of her had remained defiant. That defiance had gotten her up and out of the tank and built her a new body, but it didn't change the fact that a bomb had nearly destroyed her.

Lexo and Niko were talking quietly, leaving the ladies in a bubble of privacy.

Stitch whispered, "Did you really run into the Splice?"

"Twice. I have to commend you on your choice of built-ins for Lexo. He is very effective."

"He was always good with his hands. How could you be attacked twice?"

Alphy wrinkled her nose. "I think they tracked my signal. It was almost as if they were looking for me."

Stitch stared and then nodded.

"Right. The abduction. If they did something to your brain, you might be summoning them without knowing it."

"I think it was more of an afterthought. They came here and then found me. Nothing more. I found out what I was made of, and so did Lexo."

Stitch pursed her lips. "So, what about you and my brother?"

"What about it?"

"Are you interested?"

"Sure, but I need Lucky to build me a new subroutine. I feel the interest, but my body doesn't react. It is all emotional for the time being, and Lexo says he is willing to wait."

"Wait, so you want to, but your body doesn't have the right programming?"

Alphy smirked. "The nanites are built for survival and to mimic human tissue. My brain is holding them together, so I need either my brain or the machines to be able to act without conscious thought.

It is either that, or we can wait ten years until I regenerated a bit of tissue. That might help."

Stitch snorted. "Right. We are going to find Lucky. I don't want either of you to go mad from frustration before this situation is ratified. Priorities are in place."

Alphy hugged her and whispered, "You always were good at assessing a situation and figuring out what would make it work."

Stitch hugged her back. "Yes, but I never thought it would pertain to my brother's sex life."

They pulled away at arm's length and then giggled. Alphy's brain rejoiced. She had one friend back, and now, she just had to collect the others. If she couldn't have her family, she would take what she could find. Friends were better. Friends were chosen.

She chose to find them and bring

them to the closest thing to home. With her.

<h1 style="text-align:center">Epilogue</h1>

"Is everyone settled?" Alphy sat in the captain's chair.

Niko nodded. "They are all in their quarters."

"Are all medical patients taken care of?"

Stich chuckled and reported. "They are all strapped down, some for fun, some for practical purposes."

Alphy grinned. "Set the course for Khiron Station."

Lexo replied, "Course set."

"Deploying monitoring and defensive satellites." Alphy narrowed her eyes as she protected the base and its crew of six waiting for their return.

"Right, lady and gentlemen, let's go." She paused and watched as Lexo's hand hovered over the control button. "Punch it."

"Aye, Captain." Lexo's grin was in his voice as he turned the ship and they began to build speed at an amazing rate.

They were off to collect Lucky. Who knew what she had been up to in the interim? Hopefully, she had been having a better time than Alphy. They would know soon enough. Khiron Station was four days away.

Author's Note

Sorry for the delay, life is a funny thing. Here is hoping I can get to book three by the end of the year. ☺

Thanks for reading.

Viola Grace

About the Author

Viola Grace (aka Zenina Masters) is a Canadian sci-fi/paranormal romance writer with ambitions to keep writing for the rest of her life. She specializes in short stories because of the thrill of discovery, of all those firsts, is what keeps her writing.

An artist who enjoys a story that catches you up, whirls you around and sets you down with a smile on your face is all she endeavours to be. She prefers to leave the drama to those who are better suited to it, she always goes for the cheap laugh.